HENRYK SIENKIEWICZ.

FOR DAILY BREAD

And Other Stories

BY

HENRYK SIENKIEWICZ

AUTHOR OF "QUO VADIS," "PAN MICHAEL,"
"WITH FIRE AND SWORD," "HANIA,"
"LET US FOLLOW HIM," ETC.

TRANSLATED FROM THE POLISH
BY IZA YOUNG
The Translator of "*Without Dogma*"

Fredonia Books
Amsterdam, The Netherlands

For Daily Bread And Other Stories

by
Henryk Sienkiewicz

ISBN: 1-58963-523-X

Reprinted from the 1898 edition

Fredonia Books
Amsterdam, The Netherlands
http://www.fredoniabooks.com

CONTENTS

FOR DAILY BREAD

**A Story from the Life of American
Emigrants**

FOR DAILY BREAD.

I.

THE VOYAGE.

A German steamer, the "Blücher," from Hamburg, was on her way to America.

It was the fourth day of her voyage and the second since she had left the green shores of Ireland behind and was on the open sea. From her deck, as far as the eye could reach, nothing was to be seen, but an expanse of greyish-green water, ploughed into deep, foam-crested furrows, getting darker in the distance and melting into the horizon covered with fleecy clouds.

The reflection of the clouds lent here and there a pearly tint to the water, on the background of which the black hull

3

stood out in sharp distinct lines. Her
head was toward the West and she rose
and fell steadily with the waves; at
times she seemed to disappear altogether
and then again rose almost clean out of
the water. Waves went to meet her
and she went towards the waves cutting
them in two with her bow. A long
streak of churning, milky water trailed
like a serpent behind and a few seagulls
followed screaming in her wake.

The wind was favorable, the ship was
going at half speed and had hoisted all
her canvas. The weather seemed to
improve steadily, and long rifts of blue
sky appeared between the ragged clouds.
There had been a strong wind blowing
ever since the "Blücher" left Hamburg,
but no gale. The wind was due west,
but fell at intervals; then the sails came
down with a heavy flapping sound but
soon filled again. Sailors dressed in
blue jerseys tightened or slackened the

ropes with the monotonous chanting of
"Yo-hoy! Yo-hoy!" stooped and rose in
time to the doleful tune, which mingled
with the boatswain's shrill whistle and
the fitful puffing and breathing of the
funnel.

Attracted by the improving weather,
most of the passengers had come on
deck.   There were the dark overcoats
and hats of the first-class passengers; on
the forecastle the motly crowd of steerage passengers, mostly emigrants. Some
sat on benches with short clay pipes between their lips, others were stretched
out at full length looking down into
the water.

Several palefaced women with children in their arms, and tin mugs fastened to their belts crouched wherever
there was room.   Young men, steady-
ing themselves with difficulty, walked
up and down and staggering at every
step, sang: "Wo ist das deutsche Vater-

land?" and may be thought that most likely they would never see that Vaterland again, but nevertheless looked cheerful enough.

At a little distance from all these people stood two, who seemed more lonely and sadfaced than the others; an elderly man and a young girl. They did not speak German, hence their solitude among strangers. They were Polish peasants.

The man's name was Laurence Toporek, and the girl, his daughter, Marisha. They were going to America and had only now come on deck for the first time. On their faces, yellow from recent sickness, was an expression of mingled terror and astonishment. They looked around with frightened eyes, at their fellow-passengers, at the sailors, the panting funnel, and the big waves which sent heavy spray and foam over the gunwales. They did not dare to speak even to each other. Laurence clutched at the railing with one hand, holding his square cap with the other, lest the wind should carry it away; Marisha held fast to her father, and when the ship heaved more violently she clung closer to him, uttering low exclamations of terror. After sometime the old man broke the silence:

"Marisha!"

"Yes, Dad?"

"Dost thou see all that?"

"Yes, I see."

"Art astonished?"

"I am, Daddy."

But she was still more terrified than astonished at what she saw, and old Toporek the same. Fortunately for them, the waves grew less in size, the wind fell altogether, and the sun burst through the clouds. When they saw the sun once more they felt cheered and comforted, and thought it were the same as shone at home. Everything was strange and new to them, and only the life and warmth giving orb seemed an old friend and benefactor.

In the meantime the sea had grown smoother. At the shrill whistle from the upper deck, the sailors nimbly climbed the rigging to furl the sails. The sight of these men hanging in mid air impressed the two with awe.

"Our lads could not do that," said the old man.

"If the Germans can do it, ours could. Jan could do it," relied Marisha.

"Which Jan, Sobkoff?"

"No, not Sobkoff. Jan Smolak, the groom."

"He is a smart lad, I know, but put him out of thy head Marisha. Thou art going to be a lady, and he is nothing but a groom, and not likely to be anything more."

"He has got his own bit of land."

"He has—at Lipincé."

Marisha was silent after that and thought with a longing sigh, if Heaven had decreed it, all would come right in the end. The sails had been furled and the screw began to churn the waters, and the heaving of the ship had almost ceased. In the distance the sea looked smooth and blue.

People began to come up more and more from the steerage quarters: laborers, German peasants, idlers and vagrants from different towns, all in search of a fortune—but not of work; the deck became crowded, therefore Laurence and his daughter, so as not to be in in anybody's way, went to the farthest end of the bows and sat down on a coil of rope.

"Dad, shall we be on the water much longer?" asked Marisha.

"How can I know? If I speak to anybody they stare at me and don't

seem to understand a Christian language."

"And how shall we be able to make
ourselves understood in America?"

"Did they not tell us that out there
are thousands of our people?"

"Daddy!"

"What is it?"

"It is all very strange and wonderful, but it is best at home, at Lipincé."

"Don't talk nonsense, child!"

After a while Laurence added as if
to himself:

"It is the will of God."

Tears sprung to the girl's eyes and
then both grew silent and thoughful,
their minds wandering back to the past.
Laurence pondered how it had come to
pass he was on his way to America. It
had happened in this way. Some six
months before his cow had strayed into
a neighbors field, and been impounded.
The man who had taken the cow claimed

three roubles for the damage done to
his clover. Laurence refused to pay,
and they went to law. The case did
not come on for some time. The neighbor did not claim damages alone, but
also for the keep of the cow, and the
costs grew larger every day. Laurence
was obstinate and did not like parting
with the money. He had spent a good
deal already on the law suit, which
dragged on for a long time, the ex-
penses increasing steadily. At last Laurence lost his case. He owed the Lord
knows how much for the cow already;
and as he had not money enough to pay
the full claim, they took his horse, and
sentenced him to a term of imprison-
ment for resisting the law. Toporek
writhed in despair. The harvest was
at hand, when he and his horse would
be wanted. He was late with his crops,
the rain ruined the grain; all this
through the bit of damage in a neigh-

bor's field.   All his money had gone,
his harvest was ruined, and beggary
stared him in the face.

As he had been a well-to-do peasant,
lucky so far in all his ventures, he grew
desperate and began to drink.   At the
inn he fell in with a German, who under
pretext of buying flax, persuaded people to emigrate.   The German began
telling him wondrous things about
America, and said that he could there
get more land than the whole village
owned, together with pasture-land and
woods.   Toporek's eyes sparkled with
anticipation.   It was too good to be
true, and he would not have believed
it, had not the dairy-farmer, a Jew,
confirmed the German's tale, and said
he knew from his nephew that land
could be got from the government for
the asking.   The German dangled great
estates before his eyes.   They tempted
the man until he was fairly caught.

Why should he stop here? Had he not already lost as much money as would have enabled him to keep a helper? Should he wait here until the last of the property was gone and then take the beggar's staff and sing at the church doors? "No! we have not come to that," he thought, and grasped the German's hand; sold out at Michaelmas, took his daughter, and here he was on his way to America.

But the journey had depressed him not a little. To start with, they had fleeced him at Hamburg; on the ship, he was one among a crowd of steerage passengers. They pushed him out of the way like a thing of no account and mocked at the language they could not understand. At dinner time, when all swarmed round the cook with their tin mugs, they were crowded out and often went hungry. The heaving of the ship and sight of that great waste of water

terrified them.   They were ill-at-ease
and lonely among a crowd of strangers.
Beside God's protection there was no
other.   Laurence tried to look uncon-
cerned before his daughter.   With his
cap put jauntily on one side, he bade
her look at things and marvel; he himself marvelled at what he saw, but at
the same time his heart quaked with
fear lest those heathens, as he called
his fellow passengers, should throw him
into the water, or make him change his
faith, or sell his soul to the evil one.

That very ship that went on churning
the water night and day, breathed and
panted like a living thing, and like a
dragon trailed behind her a hail of fiery
sparks seemed to him an unholy thing.
These childish fears, though he did not
acknowledge them before his daughter,
weighed heavily on his heart; for this
Polish peasant, torn away from his
homely nest, was verily a mere helpless

child with nobody but God to protect
him.   He could neither understand nor
take in what he saw, and sitting with
bowed head on the coil of rope, his
heart full of nameless trouble, he heard
the wind whistle the name of "Lipincê!
Lipincé!" The sun looked down at him
and said: "How goes it Laurence? I have
been in Lipincé."   But the screw went
round and round and churned the water,
and the smokestack breathed and panted
like two evil spirits that dragged him
further and further away from home.

Other memories, like seagulls following the ship, fluttered around Marisha.
Her thoughts carried her back to a quiet
evening, shortly before their departure,
when she went to the well to draw
water.   Raising the heavy crane she
sang:

> " Jan was driving his team
> Whilst Kasia went to the well."

It was a sad little voice not unlike

the howling of the swallows before setting out for their long journey. From
the verge of the wood came a long
whistle. It was Jan Smolak's signal
that he had seen the crane moving.

Presently the dull thud of horses,
hoofs was heard, and then he himself
appeared, jumped from the foal and
what he said seemed to her now like
some far off music. She shuts her eyes,
and listens again to Jan's trembling voice
"If thy dad proves obdurate, I shall
throw up my place, sell the cabin, the
bit of land, and follow thee. Marisha,
where thou art, I shall be; as the birds
fly towards the sun, I will fly unto thee;
I will sail down the stream like the wild
drake, or like the gold ring roll down
the road until I find thee, my own.
How could I live without thee Mary?
Thy ways will be my ways, what happens to thee will happen to me, in life
and death we will be one: and as I have

vowed here before the well, may God
desert me, if I desert thee, my own
love."

Recalling these words Marisha saw
before her the old well, the red moon
rising beyond the woods, and the manly
figure of Jan vowing to be faithful.

These thoughts carried hope and comfort to her heart. Jan was firm and
steady and she believed he would do as
he promised. How she wished he were
here listening to the sound of the waves.
They would not feel so forlorn; he was
not afraid of anything and always found
a way out of every difficulty. What
was he doing now at Lipincé? The first
snow must have fallen by this time.
Has he gone to the woods with his axe
or is he busy with the horses? Maybe
they sent him off somewhere with the
sledge, or he was cutting holes in the
ice on the pond? Where was her sweetheart now? And the girl saw the pic-

2

ture of the village: the hard snow creak-
ing under the heels of the passers-by ;
the ruddy glow shining through the leaf-
less branches, and rocks flying overhead
with their loud monotonous croaking,
the smoke curling up from the chimneys,
and in the distance, the woods pow-
dered with snow, reflecting the red light
of the setting sun.

Heigho! and where was she? Where
had her father's will carried her? As
far as the eye could see nothing but
water, ploughed into greenish, foam-
crested furrows, and on these immense
waters this lonely ship like a stray bird;
the sky above, a watery desert below,
the sound of wind and waves around
them, and before them, maybe, the end
of the world.

Jan, poor laddie, will you find her
even if you could skim through space
like a falcon, or breast the ocean like a
fish; do you think of her in the distant
village?

Slowly the sun began to sink and dipped into the ocean. On the rippled surface of the water appeared a broad shining path skimmering and glittering with the ever changing motion, then suddenly flamed up and lost itself in the distance. The ship, entering into the fiery path, seemed to rush on in pursuit of the vanishing sun.

The smoke coming from the funnel became red, the sails and moist lines changed into pink, and the sailors began to sing. The glowing orb became larger and dipped lower into the sea. Presently only half of it was visible, then a half-circle of shooting flames, and the whole west appeared like a great conflagration without distinction of sky or water; the waves murmured gently as if saying their evening prayer.

At such moments the human soul has wings; long forgotten memories come back in crowds, lost loves hover around and we go to meet them.

Laurence and Marisha both felt like
this, though they were like leaves torn
from the tree which has its roots deep
in the soil. Their thoughts are not in
the future but in the past. They go
back to the lanes waving with golden
corn where the thatched cabins shaded
with lime-trees are dotted about; back to
the soil, the great mother of all, who
nourished them lovingly, honest and beloved above all others on earth. That
what their simple hearts had never felt
before, they felt now. Laurence took
off his cap and the last rays of the sun
shone on his grey hair; his brain was
working how to clothe in words and tell
his daughter what he felt, at last he
said:

"Marisha! it seems to me as if we had
left everything on the other side of the
water."

"Aye, our life we left there and our
hearts," she replied in a low voice, and

raising her eyes the lips moved as if in silent prayer.

It had grown dark. The passengers gradually disappeared below, but there was still an unusual stir on deck. After a fine sunset often comes a stormy night. The officers' whistle sounded continually and the sailors hauled in the ropes. The last purple light vanished from the water and at the same time a mist rose; the stars twinkled in the sky and then disappeared. The mist grew thicker every minute and gradually veiled the sky, the horizon, and the very ship. The only visible thing was the smoke-stack and the main-mast; the figures of the sailors looked like shadows in the distance. An hour later everything was wrapped up in a white shroud, even the lantern on the ship's mast and the sparks flying from the funnel.

The ship did not roll any more. It seemed as if the waves had been crushed and smoothed under the weight of the mist.

The night came on very dark and quiet. Presently, amid the stillness there came mysterious whispers from all directions, then a heavy breathing as from a gigantic breast drawing nearer and nearer. At times it seemed as if a voice was calling out in the darkness, then more voices wailing plaintively in the distance. The voices are drawing nearer towards the ship.

The sailors hearing them say the storm calls the winds from the nether world.

The warnings became more distinct. The Captain dressed in oilskins stood on the quarterdeck; the first mate took his usual position near the compass. The passengers had all gone below. Laurence and Marisha descended to their quarters. It was very quiet there. The lamps fixed on the low ceiling

threw a dim light on the groups crouching near their berths, or close to the
wall. The room was large, but grim
looking as a fourth class waiting room.
The ceiling sloped towards the bows and
the berths at that end were more like
dark holes than sleeping places, and the
whole compartment had the appearance
of an immense cellar. The air was per-
meated with the smell of tarred ropes
and damp mouldiness. What a difference between this and a first class saloon.
A voyage of even two weeks as steerage passenger fills the lungs with poi-
sonous air, takes the healthy color out
of the face, and as often as not pro-
duces scurvy.

It was not many days since Laurence
and Marisha had come on board the
"Blücher," and yet those who formerly
had known the rosy-faced country girl
would scarcely have recognized her as
the same person. Old Laurence, too,

looked very yellow. They looked worse
than anybody else, because for the first
few days they had not dared to go on
deck; they thought it was not allowed;
they were afraid to move; how could
they know what was permitted and what
was prohibited? They sat now, like all
the others, near their belongings. The
whole place was strewn with bundles of
all shapes and sizes. Bedding, garments, provisions, and tin vessels were
distributed everywhere in little mounts;
and on these sat the emigrants, mostly
Germans. Some chewed tobacco, others
smoked pipes; the clouds of smoke
curled up to the low ceiling and dimmed
the light of the lamps. A few children wailed in the corners; but the usual
noise and racket had subsided; they all
seemed to be subdued or oppressed by
the fog. The more experienced emigrants knew a storm was coming. It
was no secret to all of them that danger

was drawing nigh, maybe death
Laurence and Marisha knew nothing
about it, though when the hatchway was
opened they heard the sinister voices
coming from the boundless space.

They were sitting near the bows,
where the annoying motion of the ship
was mostly felt, and for that reason they
had been pushed there by their com-
panions. The old man was munching
a piece of dry bread, the remnant of
provisions brought from home, and
Marisha, tired of doing nothing was
braiding her hair for the night.

After a time the dead silence, interrupted only by the cries of children,
seemed to attract her attention.

"Why are the Germans so quiet to-
day?" she asked.

"How can I know?" replied Laurence.
"Maybe it is some religious ceremony
of theirs."

Suddenly the ship rocked heavily as

if startled by a dreadful apparition.
The tin vessels on the floor clattered;
the gloomy light jumped and flared up,
and frightened voices asked:

"What was that?"

There was no answer. Another shock,
more powerful than the first, struck the
ship; the bows rose suddenly and as
suddenly fell again, and a heavy wave
came crashing against the ship's planks.

"A storm is coming," whispered Marisha, in a terrified voice. Then something roared around the vessel like the
wind among huge forest trees, or a pack
of hungry wolves in scent of a prey.
The wind struck the ship once or twice,
and laid her low, then turned her round,
raised her high, and hurled her down
into the depths. The timber creaked,
the tin mugs, kettles, and bundles were
thrown from one corner to the other.
Scattered feathers were flying round,
some people trying to steady themselves

fell down on the floor, and the lamps jingled and rattled dolefully.

Then came a roar, a heavy thud, and the splashing of waves across the deck; the ship staggered as though in a drunken frenzy, and the wailing of the children and outcries of women, mingled with the shrill whistle from the quarterdeck, and the heavy tread of the sailors.

"Holy Mother of God!" whispered Marisha.

The bows of the ship where both were crouching rose and fell rapidly and in spite of their holding on to their berths they were bruised against the beams. The roaring of the waves increased, the timber creaked and groaned, and it seemed as if at any moment the ship would go to pieces.

"Hold on fast, Marisha," shouted Laurence, so as to make himself heard amid the uproar, but terror held him by the

throat as it did the others. Even the
children left off wailing, the women did
not scream any longer, but all breasts
were heaving in silent anguish, and con-
vulsive hands clutched anything for
support.

The force of the storm was still increasing. The elements had lashed
themselves into fury; the mist was mixed
up with the darkness, the clouds with
the water, the wind with the foam.
The waves thundered against the ship
with the roar of cannons and great
masses of seething water swept over her,
fore and aft.

The oil lamps, one by one, began to
go out. It became darker and darker,
and to Laurence and his daughter it
seemed like the darkness of death.

"Marisha," began the peasant in a
gasping voice, because the breath failed
him, "Marsiha, forgive me that I led
you into destruction. Our last hour

has come. We shall never see the world
with our sinful eyes again. No holy
sacraments for us or Extreme Unction;
not for us to lie in sacred ground, but
from the waters we must rise for the
Last Judgment." When he said this,
Marisha understood that all hope was
lost. Various thoughts crossed her
mind and something seemed to cry out
aloud.

"Jan! Jan! My own, do you hear
me in far off Lipincé?"

A terrible anguish tore her heart and
she began to sob aloud. Her sobbing
became audible amid the general silence.
Somebody from a corner called out: "Be
still!" and then as if afraid of his own
voice relapsed again into silence. The
glass fell down from a lamp, and another light went out, and it became
darker still. The people huddled together, to be within reach of each other.
The awful silence still reigned unbro-

ken, when amid the general hush, the voice of Laurence rose in a quavering but sufficiently loud tone:

"Kyrie Eleison."

"Christe Eleison," responded Marisha sobbing.

"O Lord, we beseech thee to hear us."

"O Lord have mercy upon us."

They were saying the Litany.

The voice of the old man and the faltering response of the girl sounded very solemn in the darkness. Some of the emigrants bared their heads. Gradually the two voices became steadier and grew more distinct amid the roaring element which played the accompaniment.

Presently piercing screams came from those stationed near the hatchway; the door burst open, the water rushed in and flooded the compartment. The panic-stricken women climbed on the berths and each thought their last hour had come.

Upon this an officer, lantern in hand,
appeared in the door, his red face glis-
tening with moisture. He explained in
a few words that the water had come in
by accident, and that there was but little danger for the ship on the open sea.
About two hours passed. The tempest
still raged as fiercely as ever. The timber creaked and strained, the ship rose
and fell but did not founder. Another
few hours passed, and the grey dawn
peeped through the heavily barred windows. The morning light looked weird
and sad as if scared at its own appearance, but it brought hope and comfort
to the passengers. After having repeated all the prayers they knew by
heart, Laurence and Marisha crept to
their bearths and fell into a heavy sleep.

They were awakened by the sound of
the breakfast bell, but neither of them
felt any desire for food. Their heads
felt as heavy as lead; especially the old

man's, whose brain was too confused to
form a single idea. The German who
persuaded him to emigrate had told him
he would have to cross the water; but
Laurence had never dreamed there
would be so much of it, and that it
would take so many days and nights to
cross it. This idea about crossing the
water was a ferry boat in which he had
crossed the river many times. Had he
known the sea was so wide he would
never have left his native land. Besides
this, another more terrifying thought
tormented his brain: had he not brought
his soul and that of his daughter to
eternal perdition? Was it not a mortal
sin for a Catholic from Lipincé to tempt
Providence by going across that waste
of water where they had been now five
days and nights without seeing any land
at all; if there be any to be seen? His
doubts and fears tore him hither and
thither, till he could not think anymore.

The storm raged forty-eight hours and then abated. They dared once more to venture on deck, but when they saw the huge mountains of water still tossing wildly about the ship, they thought that only God's hand, or a superhuman power could save them.

At last it became fine again But one day passed after another with nothing around them but the deep waters, sometimes green, then blue, melting into the distant horizon. Clouds drifted along the sky which took red and golden hues towards sunset, and the ship seemed to be following in their wake.

Laurence thought there was indeed no limit to the water, and he resolved to try whether he could make himself understood by somebody on the ship.

He lifted his square cap and bowing very lowly, he humbly addressed a passing sailor:

"Could the gracious Pan tell me how

3

soon we might arrive at the other side of the water?"

O wonder! the sailor did not burst out laughing as the others had done when Laurence spoke to them, but stood still and listened. A puzzled expression came into his rugged face as if he tried hard to remember something long ago forgotten; after a short pause he asked:

"Was?"

"Shall we soon see land, gracious Pan?"

"Two days, two days," repeated the sailor with some difficulty, and raised two fingers, to make his meaning clearer.

"Thank you, humbly."

"Where do you come from?"

"From Lipincé."

"Was is das Lipincé?"

Marisha, who had approached during their conversation, raised her eyes timidly to the sailor, and blushingly said in a low voice:

"We come from Posen, please sir."

The sailor looked thoughtfully at the girl and her flaxen hair and something like emotion seemed to work in that rugged countenance.

After a short pause, he said gravely:

"I have been in Dantzig—I understand Polish—I am a Kashuba, your bruder—but that was long ago. Jetzt bin ich Deutsch."

Saying this, he drew at the line he held in his hand with the monotonous sailor's "Yo-hoy!"

Henceforth whenever Laurence and Marisha appeared on deck he greeted them with a friendly smile; and they rejoiced at having found a single soul on this German ship that was well disposed towards them.

Two days later when they came on deck, a strange sight met their eyes. They saw in the distance something rocking on the sea, and when the ship came

nearer, they saw it was a red-cask rocked
by the waves; in the distance appeared
another, a third, and a fourth. In spite
of a slight mist the smooth water shone
like silver and as far as the eye could
see, red casks in numbers were floating
on the surface. Seagulls with shrill
cries fluttered about the ship, and the
deck now became very lively. The
sailors began changing their jerseys,
some washed the deck, while others were
busy polishing the brasswork, or hoist-
ing the flag. Animation and joy prevailed among all the passengers who
crowded the deck, strapping together
their lighter luggage and parcels.

Seeing all this, Marisha said:

"Surely that means we are near the
end of our voyage," and both brightened
visibly.

And then in the East appeared the
island of Sandy Hook, and another island crowned with a huge building, and

further on appeared a thick mist or
cloud, like curling smoke along the shore
full of shadowy formless shapes. A
joyous murmur broke from the crowd
and many hands pointed in that direction, even the boatswain's shrill whistle
seemed to participate in the universal
joy.

"What is it?" asked Laurence.

"New York," replied the Kashuba
sailor, who stood near him.

Whilst the ship ploughed onwards,
the misty cloud seemed to grow more
transparent and roofs, chimneys, and
pointed towers to emerge from it. Below, near the town appeared a forest of
masts, their various colored flags fluttering to the breeze like so many flowers
on a meadow. The ship came nearer
and nearer—and a beautiful town seemed to rise almost out of the water. A
great joy and wonder took hold of Laurence's heart. He raised his cap, opened

his mouth, and looked and looked, then
turned to his daughter:

"Marisha! dost see all that?"

"Oh, Merciful Saviour, what a sight!"

"And dost thou marvel, Marisha?"

"I do, Daddy."

Laurence not only marvelled at what
he saw, but his eyes began to shine.
Seeing the green banks at either side
of the town and the long stretches of
wooded parks, he exclaimed:

"Well! God be praised! If they will
let me have some land close to the town;
with that meadow there, it would be
convenient to the market. Come mar-
ket-day; I take a cow, a pig or two, and
there is a ready sale. There is people
there as thick as poppy-seed. In Po-
land I was a peasant, here I shall be a
Pan (master)."

At that moment they came in sight
of the Battery Park, its whole length,
and Laurence seeing all those trees, said
again:

"I shall bow deeply before the gracious commissioner, and maybe give a hint to let me have a bit of that woodland too or at least to give me permission to gather fuel. If we are to be land owners let us have something good. Early in the mornings I should send the helper with timber to the market Praised be the Lord! I see the German has not deceived me."

Marisha also smiled at the thoughts of their great possession and what her Jan would say when he found her a great heiress.

In the meanwhile a boat with the quarantine officials approached the ship, and four or five men came on deck. Then another boat from the city itself bringing agents from hotels, boarding houses, railways, and money-changers, all these pushing and jostling each other occupied the whole deck. Laurence and Marisha did not know what to do with themselves amid that seething crowd.

The Kashuba sailor advised Laurence to change his money, and he would stand by him and see that he was not cheated. This advice Laurence followed. For the money he had, he received forty-seven silver dollars. Before all this was settled the ship had come near the town and not only were the houses plainly visible but also the wharves and the people standing there; then passing other greater and smaller ships they entered the ship's dock.

The voyage was over.

People streamed across the gangway like bees out of a hive. The first-class passengers took the lead, after them came the second class, and lastly the steerage passenger. When Laurence and Marisha, jostled by the crowd, arrived at the gangway they found their friend, the sailor, standing close by.

He grasped Laurence by the hand, and said:

"Bruder, I wish you Glück, and to you also maiden. God speed you!"

"God bless you," both said in one voice as there was no time for more words. The crowd carried them along the narrow gangway into the spacious inclosure. Officials shook and squeezed their bundles, then shouted "all right," and pointed to the door. They passed across and found themselves in the street.

"Daddy! what shall we do now?"

"We must wait here," said Laurence. "The German told me an agent from the government would come to take care of us."

And so they stood close to the wall waiting amid the noise and turmoil of the great town. They had never seen anything like it. Broad and straight streets before them crowded with

people, as if at a fair, and car-
riages, laden wagons and om-
nibuses rolling along in one incessant
stream. Workmen were shouting to
each other, vendors crying out their
wares, a very babel of unintelligent
voices. Black people with curly heads
passed them every moment. At the
sight of those, both Laurence and Marisha crossed themselves piously. They
felt utterly bewildered in a place so full
of noises, whistling of locomotives, rumb-
ling of wheels and human voices.
Everybody seemed in such a hurry, as
if running away from somebody or in
chase of something; there seemed to be
no end to the crowd and strange looking
faces, black, olive-colored or red. Where
they were standing, near the docks,
everything was in motion; bales were
taken from one ship to another, laden
carts arrived very minute, and wheel-
barrows rumbled over the bridges; there

was an everlasting noise as in a saw mill.

Thus passed an hour—and another; they still remained close to the wall, waiting for the agent.

He looked strange and out of place there, this Polish peasant, in the long, grey hair, and square, fur-cap; with the fair-haired girl, in her close fitting bodice open at the throat, with rows upon rows of beads around her neck.

People passed them without a look. Nobody here wonders at new faces or strange dresses.

Another hour passed; the sky became overcast, rain and sleet began to fall, and a cold wind blew from the water. They still waited for the agent.

The peasant is by nature patient and much enduring, but his heart began to fail him.   It had been lonesome enough on board ship among strangers and surrounded by that immensity of water. They had prayed to God to lead them

safely across the watery desert. They
thought if they once touched land again
they would be safe. And here they were in
a great town amid noisy crowds, lone-
lier and more terrified than when on
board ship.

What should they do if the agent
did not come at all, if the German had
told them what was not true?

At the very thought their simple
hearts beat faster, they would be lost
indeed.

And the wind grew colder and the
rain soaked through their clothing.

"Marisha, art thou cold?" asked Laurence.

"Yes, Daddy, very cold," whispered
the girl.

The town clocks again struck the
hour. It was getting dusky. The
movement in the wharves slackened, the
lamps were lit and a stream of glaring
light filled the street. The dock-labor-

ers in lesser or greater groups, singing
and shouting, marched past them towards their homes and rest. They had
nowhere to go, the cold pierced their
bones, and they began to feel very hungry. If they had only a roof over their
heads to shelter them from the rain—
and the agent did not come.

Poor Laurence, poor Marisha, there
are no such things as agents to look after
stray emigrants. The German was
agent for a steamship company that paid
him a commission of so much per head
for every emigrant. It was his business
to send as many on board ship as he
could and he did not trouble himself
about anything else.

Laurence felt that his feet were giving way, a great weight seemed to press
him down to the earth; it must be the
wrath of God which hung over him, he
thought.

"Daddy!"

"Hush! be quiet, there is no mercy for us."

"Daddy! Let us go back to Lipincé."

"Let us go and drown ourselves!"

"O, Merciful God!" whispered Marisha.

Laurence's heart was suddenly stirred with compassion.

"Poor orphan! If the Lord would only show mercy to thee."

But Marisha did not hear his words; her eyes had closed and she slept. Feverish dreams carried her back to Lipincé, and she heard Jan, the groom, singing:

"'Tis a great, great lady, my blue-eyed Sue,
All her possessions, a garland of rue"

The pale morning light in the New York docks fell upon the masts, the water, and the emigrant building. Then it touched gently two figures sleeping under the wall. Their faces looked pale, and thick flakes of snow were clinging to their garments.

II

AT NEW YORK.

In New York, coming from Broadway and passing Chatham Square, in the direction of the river, one crosses several streets. Here the traveler finds himself in a part of the city more and more poor, desolate, squalid, and gloomy. The streets are getting narrow; the houses, built perhaps by the early Dutch settlers, are cracked and grown crooked from extreme old age; the roofs are bent in, the plaster has peeled off from the walls, and the walls themselves have sunk only part of the windows show above the street. Crooked lines take the place of the favorite straight lines of American streets, roofs, walls, all are strangely out of shape and piled up one above the other.

Being close to the river, this part of
the city is scarcely ever dry, and the
narrow streets thickly studded with
houses are like marshes full of black,
stagnant water with all kinds of refuse
floating on its greasy surface. There
is everywhere dirt, untidiness, and human misery.

In these quarters are the boarding
houses, where for two dollars a week bed
and food may be obtained; here also are
the barrooms, where the whalers entice
all sorts and conditions of men to their
ships; here agents from Venezuela,
Ecuador and Brazil tempt the unwary
to their fever-stricken marshes; eating-
houses where they feed their customers
on salt junk, bad fish, and oysters; gamb-
ling dens, Chinese laundries, and various sailors' homes; here lastly are the
dens of crime, wickedness, misery and
tears.

And yet this part of the city is very

crowded, for all the emigrants who cannot find room in Castle Garden and will not or cannot go to the lodging houses congregate here, live and mostly die here. One might say that if the emigrants are mostly the scum of European countries, the inhabitants of this place are the scum of emigration. The people here are mostly idle, partly because they cannot obtain work and partly because they will not work. Night is made hidious by revolver shots, cries for help, hoarse yells of rage, songs of drunken brawlers, or the howling of quarreling negroes. In the daytime, prize fights and betting on the principals are the customary amusements of the inhabitants. Ragged children and curly-headed little negroes and mulattoes crowd the streets, picking up stray bits of vegetables or bananas, and imaciated begger women stretch out their

4

hands for alms if a well dressed person happens to pass by.

In this earthly Gehenna we find our old friends, Laurence Toporek and his daughter, Marisha. The lordly possession of which they had dreamed had vanished into air, and reality was before them in the shape of a narrow basement, deep in the ground, with one broken window, the walls stained with damp and black fungus, the whole furniture consisting of a rusty, battered stove, a three-legged chair, and a heap of straw which serves for a bed.

Old Laurence on his knees before the stove, is searching among the ashes for a stray potato, and he returns to this search again and again; Marisha is sitting on the straw, her hands clasped round her knees, her eyes staring on the floor. She looks ill and wan. It is the same Marisha, but the once rosy cheeks are pale and thin, the whole face is smaller, and the great blue eyes have a vacant look. Her face shows the effects of foul air and scanty nourishment.

They lived mostly on potatoes; and now even these have failed, and they do not know what to do next, nor how to live. It is three months since they came into this place and their little supply of money is gone. Laurence tried to get work, but nobody could understand what he wanted. He went to the docks ready to carry bales, or load coals into the ships, but the Irishmen drove him away.

Of what use was a laborer who could not understand what was said to him. Wherever he went, and whatever work he tried to do, he was pushed aside and laughed and jeered at for his pains. His hair had grown snow-white with sorrow, hope had left him, his money was gone, and hunger stared in the face.

At home, among his own people, even
extreme poverty would have looked different.   With staff in hand and a wallet
slung across his shoulders, he would
have stood singing near the cross on
the roadside or at the church entrance:
the lord of the manor would throw him
a coin from the carriage, the lady send
out a rosy-faced child who would look
wonderingly at the poor man and put
money into his hand; a peasant would
give him half a loaf of bread, and
other bits of meat, he would feed like
the birds that neither plough nor sow.
Besides, standing under the cross, he
would have God's protecting arms above,
around him the sky and fields, and in
the quiet stillness the Lord would hear
him singing in his praise.   Here in this
great town there was the continual noise
and rush of people always in a hurry;
it seemed like a gigantic wheel turning
round and round and crushing all that
could not come up with it.

Heigho! what a difference from his former life! At Lipincé, Laurence owned a goodish bit of land; he was elder in the village, respected by everybody and sure of his meals for the next day. On Sundays he stood before the altar with a wax candle in his hand; and here, he was the last among people, a stray dog in a strange yard; humble, trembling, and hungry.

His conscience cried out loudly: "Laurence, why didst thou leave thy home?" Why? Because God had bereft him of his senses.

The peasant has much endurance and carries his burden patiently enough, if he sees a ray of light at the end of his calvary; but Laurence knew well enough that it would be worse every day, and the sun would rise every morning to show a still greater depth of misery for himself and his child. What should he do? A rope, a prayer, and there

would be an end of it. He was not
afraid to die—but what would become
of the girl?

When he though of all this, he felt
that not only God had forsaken him,
but that he was going mad. There was
no ray of light in the darkness he saw
before him; and the greatest pain which
continually gnawed at his heart he
could not even define or give a name
to: it was homesickness. The simple
peasant yearned for his pine woods,
thatched cabins, priests, and landlords,
all of which constituted his home and
the familiar surroundings of his former
life from which he had borne himself.
away. At times he felt inclined to tear
his hair; throw himself on the floor,
howl like a chained dog or cry out—to
whom? he did not know. He is sinking under his burden and the town is
always noisy, always clamorous; he calls
to Christ: and there are no crosses on

the roads; nobody answers or hears him;
only the noise grows louder without and
the girl crouches motionless on her
straw. They sat there from morning
until night without exchanging a word
as if they were angry with each other.
What could they talk about? The open
wounds had better be left untouched.

How was it none of their countrymen
helped them. There are many Poles in
New York, but few of them who live
about Chatham Square.

In the second week after their arrival
they met two Polish families, one from
Silesia, the other from Posen, but they
were suffering themselves. The Silesi-
ans had lost two children, and with the
last surviving one had slept under the
arches of the bridges living by what
they could pick up until they were taken
to the hospital. The second family was
in a more unhappy condition because
the father was a drunkard. Marisha

had helped the woman as long as she could; now she needed help herself.

They might have gone to the Polish Church in Hoboken, and the priest would have made their case known. But they were ignorant of this, could not ask their way, and any money spent meant a step nearer to destitution.

They sat there; he before the stove, she on the straw in the room. Though it was only noon, it grew darker, from the mist arising near the water. It was warm outside but they trembled with cold; at last Laurence gave up all hope of finding anything in the ashes.

"Marisha," he said, "I cannot bear it any longer. I will go and see whether I can pick up any wood and maybe find something to eat."

She said nothing in reply, and he went out. He had acquired some practice by this time and knew how to catch the driftwood which the tide brings near the

docks. Many of those who have no
money with which to buy coal do the
same.   Often he got kicked and driven
away, but now and then he found pieces
of wood or something to eat, besides the
eagerness of his search made him forget his hard fate and the ever present
pain of homesickness.   When he reached the dock it was luncheon time, the
men had gone away, and the smaller
boys, though they pelted him with mud
and oyster shells could not drive him
away.   Pieces of wood were rocking on
the water, one wave brought them near,
another carried them back, but he managed to secure a good supply nevertheless.   Other light objects were floating
in the distance out of his reach.   The
boys threw lines and drew them on the
shore.   He had no line, so he waited
until the boys were gone, then looked
over what they had left and picked out
what he could eat.   It never even

crossed his mind that his daughter was hungry.

Fortune befriended him this time. On his way back he saw a cart laden with potatoes stuck fast in the mud. Laurence put his shoulder to the wheel, and helped the driver to get it out. It was heavy work, but he strained all his muscles, the horses gave a hard pull and the cart got loose. As it was heaped full a great many potatoes rolled off in the mud. The driver did not stop to pick them up, he thanked Laurence for his help, shouted to the horses, and drove on.

Laurence knelt down and gathered them with trembling hands and his heart grew hopeful once more. Wending his way homewards, he murmured to himself:

"Praised be the Almighty, he has answered my prayers. The lassie will light the fire, there is wood enough, and

potatoes to last us two days. The Lord
is merciful! The room will look more
cheerful, and poor Marisha will be glad.
God is merciful!"

Muttering thus, he went along, carrying the wood and feeling now and then
whether the potatoes were safe. He
had a great treasure, therefore he raised
his eyes in gratitude to heaven, and
again muttered:

"I thought nothing remained for me
but to steal some food—and here it fell
from the cart like a gift from heaven.
We were without food, now we have
plenty. God be praised. Marisha will
jump up from the straw when she hears
the news."

In the meanwhile Marisha had not
changed her position. At times when
Laurence brought wood, she had made
the fire, brought water, and eaten what
there was and then sat down again staring silently at the blaze. She, too, had

endeavored to find work. They had
taken her on in one of the boarding
houses to sweep the rooms and wash
the dishes; but as they could not make
her understand and she often did the
wrong thing from not understanding
what they wanted, they sent her away
after two days' trial. Now she sat the
whole day in the house afraid to go into
the street because drunken sailors often
stopped her on the way. This enforced
idleness made her still more unhappy.
Homesickness was eating into her soul
like rust into iron. She was far less
happy than Laurence; for besides hunger and the hopelessness of their future,
the thoughts of her lost love was always
with her. Jan had promised and vowed:
"Where thou goest I will go," but she
had hoped to become a lady, and now
everything was changed.

He was head groom at the Manor and
owned his own land: and she was now

a poor, hungry outcast. Would he still
follow her, take her into his strong arms
and say: "Poor, tired birdie, come to
me, or would he cast her off as a pauper's
daughter?" The dogs would bark at
her in Lipincé, as they do at vagrants
and beggars; and yet the wish of her
soul was to be there once more; to live
near him, even if he spurned her.

When they had a fire and hunger was
not so near, she saw pictures of past
days in the glowing embers. She saw
herself, sitting at the spinning wheel
with other girls around her. Jan had
crept up behind and whispered into her
ear: "Marisha we will go the priest together, for thou art very dear to me."
And she had stopped her ears and
thrown her apron over her head in confusion but listened to it all the same and
felt so lighthearted and happy. Another
time he had dragged her forth from the
corner where she was hidden and asked

her to dance with him and she had
turned her head away and bade him go
away she felt so ashamed and bashful.
She had seen it all over and over again
in the crackling flames through eyes
dimmed with tears; now there was
neither fire nor tears, both had burned
out, but though her eyes were dry the
tears were burning deep down in her
heart. She felt very tired and very
weak; but she suffered patiently and
humbly, and there was an expression in
the large blue eyes like a dumb animal
that is tortured.

Thus she looked now sitting on the
straw. Somebdy moved the latch of
the door; she thought it was her father
and did not raise her head, then a rasp-
ing voice called out:

"Look here!"

It was the owner of the tumble-down
rookery they lived in; a mulatto with
a dirty, scowling face, and a chew of
tobacco in his mouth.

When the girl saw who it was she felt frightened. They owed him the week's rent in advance and they had not a cent. She thought humble entreaty might prevail with the man. She approached him, and gently kissed his hand.

"I have come for the dollar," he said.

She understood the word dollar, and shook her head, and looking at him supplicatingly, she tried to make him understand that they had no money left and had had no food for nearly two days.

"The good God will reward you," she said in her own tongue, not knowing what to do or what to say.

The mulatto only understood that no dollar was forthcoming, and taking her bundle with one hand and the girl with the other he pushed her into the street, throwing down her things beside her; then with the same stolidity, he opened

the door of the barroom close by, and
called out:

"Hi, Paddy! there is a room for you!"

"All right," responded a voice from
within, "I will come to-night."

Presently the mulatto disappeared
within the dark entrance and Marisha
remained standing alone in the street.
She placed her bundles into a sheltered
corner to keep them clean, and stood
close by them, humble and patient.

The passers-by left her unmolested.
It had been dark in the room but the
street was still comparatively light and
in that light the girl's face looked pale
and warm as if she had risen from a
sick-bed. The light flaxen hair was the
same, but the lips were pale; the eyes
sunken in and encircled with bluish
rings; the cheekbones very prominent.
She looked like a faded blossom, or a
girl in the last stages of consumption.

The passers-by looked compassionate-

ly at her. An old negress asked her a
few questions, but receiving no reply,
went on her way feeling offended.

In the meantime Laurence was on his
way back, full of that kindly feeling
which in very poor people is roused by
a manifest sign of God's providence.
He now had potatoes, he thought, and
they would eat. The next day he would
go out again to look after wagons; and
after that, well, he did not think further ahead—he was too hungry. When
he saw the girl standing on the pavement he wondered and quickened his
steps.

"Why art thou standing in the
street?"

"The landlord has turned us out,
Dad."

"Turned us out?"

He stared at her in a helpless way;
the wood fell from his hands. This was
too much for him. To turn them out

5

when he had found wood and potatoes.
He dashed his cap on the pavement,
turned round and round, stared wildly
at the girl, and repeated:

"Turned us out into the street?"

Then he seemed to be going somewhere but turned back and asked in a
hoarse voice:

"Why didst not ask him to be patient,
stupid girl?"

"I did ask him," whispered Marisha.

"Didst embrace his knees and kiss his
hand?"

"I did, Daddy."

Laurence again turned round and
round like a trodden worm; everything
seemed to grow dark before his eyes.

"A curse upon thee, for a stupid
wench."

The girl looked mournfully at him.

"It was not my fault, Daddy."

"Stop here and do not budge, I will
go and ask him to let us, at least, roast
our potatoes."

He went inside. In a few moments voices were heard, a stamping of feet, and Laurence came flying out into the street pushed evidently by a powerful hand.

For a moment he stood still, then turning to his daughter, he said abruptly: "Let us go."

She stooped to pick up the bundles, which were very heavy, but Laurence did not offer any help or take any notice that the girl was too weak to carry them.

They started off. Two such miserable beings as the old man and his daughter would have attracted the attention of any passer-by were they not so accostumed to such sights of destitution.

The girl's breathing became more and more difficult, she tottered on her feet once, then twice, and at last, said entreateningly:

"Daddy! take the bundles, I cannot carry them any longer."

"Throw them away, then."

"But the things will be needed."

"They will not be needed."

Suddenly, seeing that she hesitated, he exclaimed fiercely:

"Throw them down, or I will beat thee."

This time, the girl frightened by her father's voice and fierce eyes, obeyed, and he went on muttering to himself:

"It is fate, and there is nothing else left."

Then he became silent, but his eyes gleamed savagely. They crossed the little streets, one dirtier than the other, until they arrived near the dock, passing a building with the inscription: "Sailors' Asylum." Marisha sat down on a pile of lumber; because her feet would carry her no longer and Laurence sat beside her. The dock was teeming with life and bustle. The mist had cleared up and the warm sun-

shine fell upon the two outcasts. From
the water came a crisp breeze; there was
light and color and ever varying motion
among the big ships which with their
canvass fluttering in the wind sailed into
the harbor. Other steamers churning
the water were leaving it.

They were going home, towards Lipincé, thought Marisha, mournfully.
where they had left their happiness and
peace. How was it the Lord had forsaken them, what had they done to de-
serve such punishment? It was in His
power to bring them back; so many
ships were going out, and they were
left behind among strangers.

The tired girl's thoughts were continually hovering about the village.

"Does he still think of me," she whispered to herself, "does he remember."

She remembers, because only happiness makes us forget, but solitude and
sorrow makes us cling round the dear

ones like the tendrils of the ivy round
the oak.   Maybe he had forgotten the
old love and taken up with a new one?
Was it possible he could still think of
a poor lass who would bring him nothing but her garland of rue, who had no
possessions, and whom only death alone
would woo now.

As she was ill, hunger did not trouble her, but she felt very tired and
sleepy; she shut her eyes and the pale
face sank lower on her breast.   She
dreamed she was wandering over preci-
pices and deep ravines like Kasia in the
ballad, who fell into the Dunajelz river;
she distinctly heard the lines of the
song:

> "Jan saw her peril from the cliff above
> And threw a silken cord towards his love.
> The cord did not reach—too short by a bit
> And Kasia tied her long tresses to it."

Here she started; it seemed to her she
had no tresses and was falling into space.

The dream vanished. It was not Jan
who sat beside her, but Laurence, her
father. There was no river, only the
dock with its forest of masts, and funnels. Some ships were leaving the pier,
and thence came the singing which had
mingled with her dream. A quiet,
balmy, spring evening spread a ruddy
glow on sky and water. The river was
without a ripple and every ship and
every pile stood clearly reflected in the
water. There seemed to be peace and
happiness spread everywhere—but beyond the reach of those two waifs; the
workmen were beginning to return towards their homes, these two only had
nowhere to go.

Hunger with its iron claws began to
gnaw at Laurence's vitals. The peasant
sat there in gloomy silence, a fierce re-
solve depicted on his face. If anybody
had looked at him, he would have been
frightened at that despairingly quiet

face with the expression of a rapacious animal. He had not opened his lips to the girl since he bade her throw down the bundles; now he said in a strange voice:

"Come, Marisha."

"Where are we going?"

"To the end of the pier, near the water. We will lie down on the boards and sleep."

They crossed the long, winding pier until they reached the covered platform where during the day the workmen had been busy, but there was nobody there now.

When they reached the furthest end Laurence said:

"We will lie down here."

Marisha sunk down at once, and in spite of the swarming mosquitoes, fell into a heavy sleep.

Suddenly in the depth of night the voice of Laurence awakened her.

"Marisha, get up!"

There was something in the tone of his voice which roused her instantly.

"What is it, Daddy?"

In the midst of the stillness the old man's voice sounded hollow and terribly quiet.

"Child! never more shalt thou suffer from hunger. Thou shalt not beg thy bread at the stranger's door nor sleep under the open sky. People have abandoned us. God has forsaken us. There is nothing for us but death. The water is deep and thou wilt not suffer much."

She could not see his face in the darkness, but her eyes dilated with terror.

"I will drown thee, poor lassie, and then drown myself," he continued in that same dull, even voice. "There is neither help nor mercy for us. Tomorrow thou wilt not be hungry; tomorrow thou wilt be happier than today."

"Oh, no." she did not wish to die; she was only eighteen and clung to life and was afraid of death.   Her very soul recoiled from the thought that her body should lie at the bottom of the sea among fishes and reptiles.   A great terror and aversion shook her whole frame, and her own father speaking thus in the darkness, seemed an evil spirit.

Both his hands were resting on her thin shoulders, and still in that same unnaturally quiet voice, he went on:

"If thou shoutest nobody will hear it; I have only to push thee, and it is all over."

"I will not die, Daddy, I will not," cried out Marisha.   "Have you no fear of God? Daddy, my own Daddy, have mercy on me!   Did I ever complain of anything, did I not patiently suffer cold and hunger with you?"

His breath came quicker and quicker and his hands held her as in a vice; she still prayed to him despairingly.

"Have mercy, I am your child. Poor
and weak, and not long to live; but I
will not die, I am afraid."

She clutched his garments and kissed
the hands that tried to push her into
the dark space. But all this seemed to
excite the old man still more. His un-
natural quietness gave way to frenzy
and he began to snort and pant like a
wild beast.

The night was dark and still, nobody
could hear them because they were at
that part of the pier where even in the
daytime none except workmen ever
come.

"Help! help!" screamed Marisha.

He dragged her violently with one
hand to the brink, while beating her on
the head with the other to smother her
cries.

But the cries did not rouse any echo;
a dog only barked in the distance. The
girl was growing faint; the piece of gar-

ment she clutched unconsciously remained in her hand and Marisha was sensible she was falling.

In her fall she grasped at a beam and remained hanging over the water.

The peasant leaned over, and horrible to say, tried to unloosen her hands.

At this moment like a flash of lightning she saw before her the short Past: Lipincé, the well with the long crane, then the voyage, the terrible storm, when they said the litany together, and their miserable life at New York. But what is this she sees: A great ship is coming towards her, nearer and nearer, there is a great crowd of people and among them stands Jan with outstretched arms and above the ship the Holy Virgin, smiling at her in heavenly glory. Oh, Holy Mother! Jan, my Jan! Daddy!" she cries out, 'there is the Mother of God! The Holy Virgin!"

A moment more and the same hands

that pushed her ruthlessly over the brink
grasp her arms and with superhuman
strength drag her upon the pier. Again
she feels the boards under her feet, two
arms infold her, they are not those of
the excutioner, but of the loving father,
and her head sinks on his breast.

When she recovered from her swoon
she saw herself lying quietly near her
father; though it was dark, she could
see he was lying on his face, both arms
spread out in the form of a cross, and
his whole frame shaking with convul-
sive sobs: "Marisha," he said in broken
tones. "Marisha, my child, forgive."

The girl searched in the dark for his
hand and covered it with kisses.

"Daddy, may the Lord Jesus forgive
you, as I do."

From a silvery cloud which shone on
the horizon came out the bright moon,
and oh, wonder! Marisha saw crowds of
silver-winged angels, gliding along the

moonbeams towards her; they fanned
her face, singing in sweet, childish
voices:

> "Peace be with thee, poor tired, child!
> Storm-tossed, battered birdie, peace
> be with thee! little field-flower, so
> patient and quiet, rest in peace!"

Singing thus they scattered lilies and
rose leaves over her and little silver bells
chimed in:

> "Rest, poor girl! sleep—sleep in peace."

And she felt well, bright and peaceful and fell off to sleep.

The night faded and early dawn whit-
ened the water. Masts and funnels
seemed to emerge from the shadow and
come nearer. Laurence knelt down
bending over his daughter.

He thought she was dead. Her
slender form was motionless; her face
was very pale, and the closed eyes were
surrounded by a bluish tint. He shook

her arm but she neither moved nor
opened her eyes. Laurence felt as if
he, too, were dying; but putting his
hand close to her mouth he felt the
faintest flutter of a breath. Her heart
was beating though very feebly, and he
thought it might stop any moment. If
there came a warm sun from out of the
morning mist she may wake up, he
thought.

The seagulls circled overhead as if
they too were taking an interest in this
human tragedy. The mist gradually
dissolved under the breath of a westerly
wind which brought with it warmth and
sweetness.

Then rose the sun. The rays fell first
on the top of the scaffolding at the end
of the pier, then going lower touched
Marisha's lifeless face. With the light
around her the sweet patient face surrounded by the flaxen hair which had
become unloosened in the struggle look-

ed like that of a saint or an angel; for Marisha thought her sufferings and patient endurance had almost reached the martyr's palm.

A rosy, delightful day rose from the water, the sun grew more powerful and a gentle wind caressed the maiden's face. The seagulls whirled and circled overhead screaming as if they wanted to awaken her. Laurence took off his long coat and spread it over his daughter's feet.

Gradually the bluish tint vanished from her face and the anxiously watching father saw a faint touch of color mounting to the cheeks, she smiled once, and twice, at last opened her eyes.

Then the old man knelt down on the planks, raised his eyes to heaven, and heavy tears ran down his furrowed face.

He felt now that from henceforth the child was as the apple of his eye, the soul of his soul, a thing holy and beloved above everything on earth.

Marisha not only woke up but she felt better and more refreshed than she had done for some time past. The pure air of the harbor had filled her lungs poisoned by the foul vapor of her narrow lodgings. She had indeed come back to life again, for she sat up and called out:

"Daddy! I am very hungry."

"Come, little daughter," said the old man, "we will go to the other end of the pier and find something to eat."

She rose without much effort, and followed him. This day was evidently to be a turning point in their fortunes for scarcely had they gone a few steps when they saw lying between two beams a red handkerchief tied up in a bundle, which on examination was found to contain some bread and meat, and a piece of pudding. Who had put it there? A laborer most likely who had eaten only a portion of his lunch yesterday. They

6

often do. Laurence and Marisha explained it in their own simple way.
Who had put it there? He, who remembers and feeds the sparrows on the
roof and the flowers in the field.

God!

They said a short prayer and ate what
they found; it was not very much for
two hungry people, but they felt refreshed and strengthened, and went
along the water front towards the larger
docks. Reaching the Emigrant Office,
they turned into Water street. With a
rest now and then it took them several
hours to accomplish the journey. Why
they went in this particular direction
they did not know themselves, but Marisha fancied going that way. On their
way they met a number of carts and
wagons going towards the water front.
Water street was full of life and motion.
People were coming in all directions
from their dwellings, and hurrying to

their offices, and places of business. In one of the open doors stood a grey-haired gentleman, with long moustaches, with a young lad by his side. He stepped out, looked at the two wanderers, his moustaches twitched, and an expression of deep astonishment appeared on his face; he came a little nearer, looked again, and then smiled.

A human being smiling at them in New York was something so wonderful, nay miraculous, that both Laurence and his daughter were astonished.

The old gentleman approached them, and addressed them in their own tongue:

"Where do you come from, good people?"

If a thunderbolt had fallen from the pure sky they would not have been more taken aback. Laurence grew as white as a sheet and reeled on his feet; unable to believe his ears. Marisha recovered first, and falling to the old man's knees, which she embraced, exclaimed:

"We come from Posen, Gracious Pan!"

"And what are you doing here?"

"Nothing, gracious Pan, but suffering hunger and misery." Her voice failed, and Laurence having shaken off his bewilderment, fell at the old gentleman's feet, clutched at the lappels of his coat, kissed them raptuously and thought he clutched at a bit of heaven.

It's our own Pan, our master," he gasped out. "He will not let us die of hunger, he will protect us and save us from evil."

The young lad who was with the elderly man opened his eyes in undisguised astonishment; people began to crowd around them to see one man kneeling before another, kissing his feet, a thing unheard of in America. The gentleman grew red, and evidently an-

gry, and turned sharply on the by-
standers:

"What are you staring at? It's none
of your business," and then turning to
Laurence and Marisha, he said:

"We cannot stand here in the street,
come with me."

They followed him to the nearest res-
taurant, and there he went with them
into a private room. Here the two
peasants again begun to embrace his
knees but he waived them off and muttered in grumpy tones:

"There, there, have done with your
foolishness! We come from the same
country, and are children of the same
mother."

The smoke of his cigar seemed to
have got into his eyes because he rubbed
them vigorously with his fist, then asked:

"Are you hungry?"

"We have eaten nothing for two days,

but what we found to-day near the
water."

"William," said he addressing the lad,
"order some lunch to be brought in
here." Then he asked again:

"Where do you live?"

"Nowhere, illustrious Pan."

"Where did you sleep?"

"On the pier."

"Did you get turned out of your lodgings?"

"We did."

"Have you no things, nothing but
what you stand in?"

"We have not."

"And no money?"

"None."

"And what do you intend doing?"

"We do not know."

The old gentleman put further questions in a sharp, quick tone; then suddenly turning towards Marisha, he said
in a gentle voice:

"How old are you, child?"

"I shall be eighteen next Michaelmas, please, Sir."

"And you have suffered a great deal?"

Instead of answering, Marisha bent humbly down to his knees; upon which the old gentleman took to rubbing his eyes again—the smoke evidently annoyed him.

A dish of hot meat and some beer was brought in. He told them to sit down and eat, at which they demurred, saying they dared not do so in his presence. He became angry again, and called them a couple of fools, but in spite of all his impatient manner he seemed to them a very angel from heaven.

His face beamed with satisfaction when he saw them making a hearty meal. After they had finished he asked them to tell him how they had come here and all that had happened to them.

Laurence told him everything as if he had been in the confessional, he had tried to drown his child; the old gentleman jumped up in a terrible rage, and fairly shouted:

"I could flay you alive for that."

Then turning to Marisha, he said:

"Come here, child."

When she approached he took her head in both his hands and kissed her on the forehead.

After a short and thoughtful pause he said:

"You have undergone great suffering and privation.   Nevertheless it is a good country for those who know how to shift for themselves."

Laurence opened his eyes in silent amazement: this good and wise gentleman called America a good country.

"Yes, you blockhead," he said, seeing Laurence's astonishment, "it is a good country.   I came here with empty pockets and have now a good income. But you peasants have no business to come out here, you ought to stick to your land, if you leave the country who is to remain there. You cannot do much here. It is easy enough to come but very difficult to get home again."

He remained silent a few minutes, and then said, as if to himself: "It's forty years since I came here, time almost to have forgotten the old home; but the longing for it comes back now and then. William must go there and get acquainted with his father's country."

"This is my son," he said, pointing to the lad.

"William you will bring me from thence a handful of soil to put under my head in the coffin."

"Yes, father," replied the lad, in English.

"And upon the breast, William, upon the breast."

"Yes, father."

The smoke of the cigar seemed to have got into his eyes again, so that they were suffused with tears. He shook himself and said gruffly:

"The rascal understands Polish well enough, but prefers to speak English. Such is fate. Where the sapling is transplanted there it grows. William, go and tell your sister that we have guests for dinner and for the night."

The lad jumped up quickly, and went out to do his bidding.

The old gentleman sat silent evidently lost in meditation, then spoke as if to himself:

"If I were to send them home it would cost a great deal, and they have nothing to go back to. Sold their property and all their sticks, nothing but a beggar's life to await them there. To send the girl into service, the Lord knows what might become of her. Since they are

here they might as well try to work.
I will send them to a settlement, the
girl will get married at once. They will
earn some money, and can go back if
they wish to, and take the old man with
them."

Then he turned to Laurence:

"Did you hear about our settlements
here?"

"No, gracious Pan, I have heard nothing."

"Oh, people, how can you come here
not knowing where to turn; no wonder
you came near perishing miserably. In
Chicago there are twenty thousand like
you; in Milwaukee as many; in Detroit
and Buffalo a great number. They work
mostly in factories, but the peasant loves
the soil best. I might send you to Radom, in Illinois, h'm! but land is more
difficult to obtain there. They are building a new Posen in the prairies at Ne-
braska, but that is too far, and the rail-

road fare is too much. St. Mary's in Texas is also too far. Barovina would be the best, especially, as I can get you free passes, and what money I give you, you can keep for other purposes.

He thought again, deeply.

"Listen to me, old man," he said suddenly. "They are opening a new settlement called Borovina, in Arkansas. It is a beautiful country, good climate and you can obtain one hundred and sixty acres, or more, of good woodland by making a small payment to the railway company. Do you understand? I will give you some money to start with, besides the railway tickets; these will take you to Little Rock, and from there you go by wagon. You will find many others there bound for the settlement. I shall provide you with letters of introduction. I will do for you what I can, because we are children of the same mother, but I am more sorry for your

daughter than for you. Do you understand?" Then his voice grew soft and
tender.

"Now listen, child," he said to Marisha," take my card, and do not lose
it. If ever you are in need of a friend,
come straight to me and I will protect
you. If I should not be alive, William
will help you. Do not lose the address,
and now, come with me."

On the way he bought for them a
change of clothes and some linen, and
then took them to his house. They
were all good people there. William
and his sister Jenny made them as welcome as if they had been relatives.
William treated Marisha as if she were
a lady, to the great confusion of the
simple girl. In the evening some young
girls, prettily dressed, with fringes on
their foreheads came to see Jenny. They
took Marisha among them, wondered at
her pale face and beautiful flaxen hair

and laughed at her timid ways and her
wanting to kiss their hands. The master of the house walked to and fro among
them, shook his white head. Sometimes
muttering to himself, addressing the
company either in Polish or English; he
talked about the far off country to Marisha and Laurence, dwelt upon stories
of the past, and the smoke of his cigar
seemed to trouble his eyes for he wiped
them frequently.

When they retired for the night, Marisha was deeply moved, seeing that
Jenny with her own hands prepared the
bed she, Marisha was to sleep upon. Oh,
how good they were! But it was not
astonishing after all, did not the gentleman come from the same part of the
country?

The third day Laurence and his
daughter were on their way to Little
Rock. The peasant felt his one hundred dollars in his pocket, and his past

sufferings seemed to him a dream; and
this was real life at last. Marisha pondered over the wonderful ways of Providence and thought that He who had
saved them from such misery would further protect them, bring Jan out to her,
and allow them to go back to Lipincé.

Towns and farms seemed to fly past
them. How different it was from New
York. There were fields and woods as
far as the eye could see, houses surrounded by trees, large tracts of waving
cornfields, just as it was at home. At
the sight of this Laurence's chest ex-
panded and he felt inclined to shout
and sing for joy. On the meadows
herds of cattle and sheep were grazing;
on the verge of the wood, men were
busy plying their axes. The train went
further and further, and the country
gradually became less settled. The
farms disappeared and the large, solitary prairie met their eyes. The wind

moved the tall grasses and wild flowers.
Here and there like a golden ribbon
twisted in and out, appeared an abandoned car track now covered with yellow flowers. The feathery heads of
grasses, mullein, and thistles seemed to
nod in welcome to the wanderers.
Hawks hung motionless in mid air looking down on the prairie. The train
rushed on as if it wanted to follow the
prairie where it lost itself in the distant
horizon.

From the windows flocks of hares and
prairie dogs could be seen; sometimes
the antlered head of a deer was seen
above the grasses. Nowhere, either
towns, churches, farms, or houses; only
stations between the stations, not a living soul. Laurence looked and looked
and could not understand how it was so
much good soil remained uncultivated.

A day and a night passed in that way.
In the morning they found themselves

in the woods. The thick trees with
vines and creepers twisted across their
branches, made a green, almost impenetrable wall on either side. Strange
birds were now and then flitting in and
out the luxuriant vegetation. Laurence
and Marisha fancied they saw among
the thicket strange riders with feathered
headgear and faces like burnished cop-
per. Seeing these vast prairies and in
penetrable woods in succession passing
before their eyes, Laurence would now
and then ejaculate:

"Marisha!"

"Yes, Daddy."

"Isn't it all wonderful?"

They at last crossed a river which
seemed to them immense. Later on
they were told it was the Mississippi;
and late at night they arrived at Little
Rock.

Here they were to ask their way to
Borovina.

7

We will leave them here. The second part of their wanderings is finished. The third will take place amid the noise of the axe, and the heavy work of the settlement. Whether there is to be less suffering, fewer tears, and less ill-fate, time will show.

III.

THE NEW SETTLEMENT.

What was Borovina. A settlement
in embryo. The name had been fixed
upon, that was the main thing; as a
name implies an existing fact and in-
spires confidence. Polish and American
newspapers published in New York,
Chicago, Buffalo, Detroit, Denver, and
Milwaukee, in fact wherever the Polish
tongue was heard, proclaimed *urbi et
orbi* generally, and especially to the
Polish settlers, that if they wished to
enjoy good health, to become rich, and
live on the fat of the land, and, maybe
afterwards, save their souls, they should
buy farms in that earthly paradise, Borovina. These announcements further
stated that Arkansas, where the new
settlement was to start into life, was as

yet sparsely settled, although the climate was most salubrious. It was true that the City of Memphis, situated on the opposite shore of the Mississippi, was a very hotbed of yellow fever; but it was a well-known fact that fever could not cross a broad river like the Mississippi; besides the Choctaws would make short work of it, as the fever trembles at the sight of a redskin. In consequence of these combinations the settlers of Borovina would have the fever district on the East, redskins on the West, they themselves living in a perfectly neutral zone.

In a few hundred years Borovina would boast of a vast population and the ground which now sold for a dollar and a half an acre would fetch a thousand dollars a square yard for building purposes.

To those who were alarmed at the proximity of Choctaws the announce-

ment stated that these noble savages
were full of friendly feeling towards
their white neighbors, especially if they
were Poles and that their mutual relations would be of the friendliest; besides
railways, and telegraph poles were sure
to frighten them away, and their disap-
pearance would be only a question of
time.

The ground had been acquired by a
railway company which would assure
the settlers with an outlet for their pro-
duce and easy communication with the
world. The announcements neglected
to state the fact that the line was only
a projected one, and was to be erected
at some future time from the sale of the
land given by the government to the
railway company. To Borovina it made
this little difference, that instead of being on a direct line it was situated in
a howling wilderness that could only be
reached by wagons, and with great difficulty.

This was a temporary inconvenience, a little disappointing for the settlers it is true, but one which would disappear in time as soon as the line was opened. Besides advertisements are not to be taken for gospel truth, and as plants transplanted to America soil grow into luxuriant leafage at the expense of its fruit, so also American advertisements spring up full blown and it is difficult to pick out the grain of truth from the rhetorical chaff. Putting aside however the humbug and puffing up of the settlement one might think it would be no worse than thousands of others whose beginning was the same and which had been praised with no less exaggeration.

The conditions from many points of view seemed favorable, therefore a great many people, spread over the States, from the great lakes to Florida, and from the Atlantic to the shores of California, applied for farms. Poles from

Prussia, Poles from Galicia, Masurs
from the plains of Warsaw, all those
that worked in the factories of Chicago
and Milwaukee and had sighed in vain
for the life which is the peasant's in-
heritance snatched eagerly at the oppor-
tunity to get back from smoke begrimed
cities to the plough. Those who felt too
hot at St. Mary's in Texas, too cold in
Minnesota, too damp in Detroit or hungry at Radom, in Illinois were eager
for a change and a few hundred people
with a fair sprinkling of women and
children started for Arkansas. They
were not deterred by the tales of the
lawlessness of the country infested with
Indians, outlaws hiding from justice,
rough squatters who despite the government's prohibition were cutting down
timber along the Red River, and the
terrible fights that were going on between the white and Indian buffalo
hunters. The Masur, if he has his

knotty stick and feels another brother
Masur at his back, is not afraid of anything. They are clannish these Masurs
from the Warsaw plains; 'like to be
within reach of each other; and work
or fight together shoulder to shoulder.

The gathering point for Borovina was
the town of Little Rock. From Little
Rock to Clarksville, the nearest settlement to Borovina, is a great distance;
and their way lay through a wild and
desolate country, heavy woods, and
swollen rivers. The few who had
started out alone were never heard of
again, but the main body arrived without mishap and were now camping out
in the woods.

To say the truth they had been very
much disappointed when they arrived
on the spot. Expecting arable land and
woods they had found nothing but a
thick almost impenetrable forest which
had to be cleared before the plough

could be used. Black oaks, redwood, cottonwood, and gloomy hickory trees, with vines and creepers as thick as cables twisting in and out, and chapparal underneath formed a solid green wall. Those who penetrated further did not see the sky above. They had to feel their way in the surrounding gloom and were in danger of losing their way and perishing in the wilderness.

One and another of the Masur lads looked at their fists, then at the huge trees,; several yards in circumference, and felt disheartened. It is well to have plenty of timber wherewith to build houses but to clear hundreds of acres before the plough could be used was a work of years.

But there was nothing else to be done; therefore on the second day after their arrival, some grasped the axe, crossed themselves, spat on their hands, and with a groan fell to work and from that time on the sound of the axe often accompanied by songs re-echoed in the woods of Arkansas.

The camp had been erected on a clearing near the river on the brink of which the future settlement was to be erected, with a school and church in the middle, the houses and cabins around them in a large square. In the meanwhile there stood the wagons forming a triangle to be used as a fortress in case of attack. Beyond the wagons grazed the mules, horses, cows, oxen and sheep under the care of young men armed with rifles. The women slept in the wagons and the men round the camp fires.

During the day only women and children stayed in the camp, the men being busy in the woods. At night wild beasts—jaguars, wolves and coyotes came from the thicket. The terrible grizzly bears which are less afraid

of fire came now and then close to the
wagons, consequently shots were often
heard in the dead of night, and shouts:
"Shoot straight at the beast." The men
who came from the wilder part of Texas
were mostly skilled hunters and provided themselves and their families with
fresh meat from antelopes, stags, and
buffalos, which were abundant in the
spring when these animals draw towards
the north. The other settlers lived on
provisions brought with them from Little Rock: Indian meal and salt pork;
beside this they killed sheep, of which
nearly every family had brought a number.

In the evenings they congregated
round the blazing camp fire, and the
young people would dance instead of
lying down to sleep. A settler who had
brought his violin played the national
dances: Obertas, Masur, and Krakoviak,
and when the sound of the violin lost

itself among the rustling of the forest, others helped it out by jingling tin plates. Time passed quickly enough amid hard work, all the harder because it was done without a system. The first thing was to build some kind of shelter, and in a short time a few log cabins, covered with bark were dotted about on the green sward. Cottonwood is easy to work but they had to go a long distance for it. Others built temporary dwellings from the canvass stripped from their wagons. Some younger men tired of felling trees began using the plough in places where the trees had been cleared and for the first time the shouts of the ploughmen were heard in the wilds of Arkansas.

Taken altogether there was such a vast amount of work to be done, that the settlers did not know where to put their hands to first; whether to build cabins, clear the forest or go hunting

for supplies of venison.   One thing was
clear from the beginning: the settlers'
agent had bought the land from the
company on faith, without taking the
trouble to examine it.   Otherwise he
could as easily have acquired a tract of
prairie land only partially wooded.   He
and the railway agent had come to the
spot in order to survey the land and
parcel out the different claims, but seeing the state of things they remained
two days, quarelled, and then under pretext of going for the surveying tools
went back to Clarksville and never
showed themselves at the settlement
again.

It soon leaked out that some of the
settlers had paid a great deal more than
others, and what was worse nobody knew
where his allotment lay or how to survey
it if they could locate it.   The settlers
had no leader or manager or any one
who was capable of adjusting their differences.

Germans no doubt would have concentrated their united strength in clearing the woods, building cabins, and after that, parcel out the claims. But each Masur wanted to work at once upon his own property, build his cabin, and prepare his own soil. Every one wanted land close to the river where the trees were fewer and water nearest. Contentions arose which grew into quarrels and free fights from the day when a certain Mr. Grünmanski made his appearance. This gentleman, who seemed to have dropped · from the clouds, came from Cincinnati, where the Germans settled; there he was known as plain Grünman, but he added the "ski" to his honest German name for business purposes.

His wagon had a high canvass roof where on either side in big black letters stood the name: "Saloon," and underneath in smaller type: Brandy, Whisky, Gin. How he had managed to· cross

the wild, lawless region between Clarksville and Borovina without having been
attasked by thieves or scalped by Indians (who in small detachments often
roam about the very neighborhood of
Clarksville) was his secret; enough that
the first day he showed himself at the
settlement he did a good business. On
that very same day the settlers began
to quarrel. To their various differences
about claims, implements, or places near
the fire, came other more trifling
grounds for disagreeing. The men became affected with provincial patriot-
ism. Those that came from the North-
ern States, praised their country at the
expense of those from the South. Loud
and angry voices in that American-Po-
lish idiom where their own mother
tongue had adopted local expressions,
were heard in the camp.

Quarrels became more virulent. It
came to fights where those coming from

the same town or settlement stood by
each other against those who came from
other parts. It was a bad lookout for
the little community who verily were
like a flock of sheep without a shep-
herd. But gradually, and by degrees,
the more experienced and wiser members of the party acquired a certain in-
fluence and authority and tried to main-
tain order. In moments of danger their
common instinct of preservation made
them forget private rancor. Once when
a party of Indians had captured some
dozen of their sheep, the lads moved
by one thought rushed after them, recovered their property, and killed one
of the Indians. That day the greatest
harmony reigned in the camp, but the
next day saw them wrangling again at
the clearings. There was also peace
and harmony when the musician began
to play their national songs, the melo-
dies they had heard under the thatched

roofs at home.   All conversation ceased,
no sound was heard but the voice of the
violin which spoke to them of the far
off country, the soughing of the wind
in the forest trees, and the crackling of
the camp fire.   With earnest, thoughtful faces, they stood around the musician, listening still, though the moon
had already risen high above the trees.
But with the exception of these peaceful
intervals the common bonds of brother-
hood were getting weaker every day.
This small community, thrown upon
their own resources without a leader,
did not know how to shift for itself.

Among the settlers we find our former friends Laurence Toporek and his
daughter Marisha, who shared the life
of the settlers.   At the beginning it
seemed to them a welcome change from
the hard pavements of New York to the
woods of Arkansas.   There they had
nothing they could call their own; here

8

they had their own wagon, some implements and live stock bought at
Clarksville. Homesickness tormented
them less among their own people, and
the heavy work did not permit them to
think much beyond of the day. The
old man was cutting trees from morning till night, and preparing timber for
his cabin. Marisha was busy washing
clothes, lighting fires, and preparing
their meals. The exercise and open
air life had effaced all traces of her illness, and her formerly pale face exposed now to the hot winds blowing
from Texas was tinged with a golden
brown. The lads from Saint Antonio
and the Lakes, who on the slightest
provocation squared their fists at each
other, agreed in one thing: that Marisha's eyes looking out from under her
silky hair were like corn flowers in a
wheat field, and she the prettiest girl
human eyes had ever beheld.

Laurence derived much benefit from
his daughter's beauty. He chose for
himself the best piece of land and nobody said him nay because all the lads
were on his side. Many of them helped
him to prepare the timber and stack it,
and the old man who was shrewd and
saw what they were aiming at, from
time to time threw out a hint:

"My little daughter," he said, "is like
a lily of the fields, a very jewel of a
girl. Some day I will choose a husband
for her from among the lads that help
me most and please me best; but he
must be a decent lad because she comes
from a decent family that owned their
own lands in the old country.

Everyone who helped him thought
he was furthering his suit. Consequently Laurence was better off than many
others and everything would have been
well with him had there been any future
for the settlement.

But things grew worse instead of better. The axe still sounded in the forest and here and there rose the yellow logs of a cabin but it was but as a drop of water in the ocean. The dark, impenetrable wall of the forest still loomed up before them showing scarcely any sign of being broken.

Those who had penetrated a little further into the thicket, reported that the forest had no limit, that awful swamps and bayous, and still, stagnant waters, full of strange creatures had impeded their march, they had heard the hissing of the serpents and strange voices calling out in warning: "Do not go further." Uncanny shrubs stretching out their branches had clutched them by their garments. A lad from Chicago swore he had seen the devil raising his hairy head from a swamp and snorting at him so fiercely that he ran for dear life back to the camp. The

men from Texas laughed at him, and
said it must have been a buffalo he had
seen, but nothing could shake his belief
that it was the evil one himself that
appeared to him. Superstition added
new terrors to their already doleful
plight. A few days later two bolder
lads ventured upon another exploration
of the woods and were never heard of
again.

People began to sicken from over-
work and fever. Quarrels and contentions grew fiercer; cattle which had not
been marked by their owners was claimed by those who had no right to them.
At last the camp broke up altogether
and the different parties shifted their
wagons as far as possible from each
other. It became evident that their
provisions would give out and hunger
stare them in the face long before anything could be expected from the soil.
Despair got hold of the people. The

sound of the axe grew fainter because
patience and courage were lacking; but
even now they would have worked if
anybody had told them "this is your un-
disputed property." As it was, nobody
knew which was his and which was his
neighbor's. They began to see that
nothing was left for them but to perish
in the wilderness. Those who still had
some money left took their wagons and
went back to Clarksville. But the
greater portion of the people had sunk
every penny they possessed in this venture and had nothing left with which
to return. These wrung their hands in
bitter despair. The axes were at last
thrown aside and the forest rustled as
if mocking at the insignificance of human efforts.

"We might go on cutting trees for
two years and then die of hunger," said
one peasant to another.

One evening Laurence came to Marisha. and said:

"It is clear that starvation is before us, we shall perish with the others."

"God's will be done," replied the girl. "He has shown us mercy before and will not desert us now."

Saying this she raised her blue eyes to the starlit heaven, and with the reflection of the fire surrounding her fair head as with a halo she looked the picture of a sweet saint.

The lads from Chicago and hunters from Texas called out:

"Marisha, our sunlight, we will stand by you."

She thought within herself that there was one only with whom she would go to the end of the world: Jan, from Lipincé. He had promised to swim across the water like a drake, to fly through the air on wings, and roll along the road like a golden ring; but he had not come, the only one she cared for had forgotten her.

Marisha had noticed long ago that the settlement was doomed, but her trust in Providence remained unshaken, and her soul purified in the fire of adversity shone serene and calm through her limpid eyes.

Beside she remembered the old gentleman at New York who had helped them before and promised to help again if they needed it.

In the meanwhile the confusion in the camp grew from bad to worse. People escaped from it in the nighttime, and what became of them it was difficult to say. And still around them the forest rustled and waved its trees and branches mocking at their helplessness.

Old Laurence fell ill from overstraining his muscles. He felt pains in his back and all his limbs. For two days he said nothing about it, the third day he could not rise from his improvised bed. Marisha went to the woods, gathered a quantity of moss and prepared for him a bed on the timber rafters which he had put together for the erection of their cabin; then set herself to concocting a cordial from various herbs and spirit.

"Marisha," murmured the old man, "death is creeping towards me from yon black forest and thou wilt remain an orphan alone in the world. God is now punishing me for my heavy sins in bringing you out here, and my last hours will be full of anguish."

"Daddy," replied the girl, "It was my bounden duty to go with you, I would not have let you come alone."

"If I left thee with a protector and saw thee married I could die easier. Marisha! take Black Orlik for thy husband, he is a good lad and will take care of thee."

Black Orlik, the great hunter from

Texas, who heard this fell on his knees before the sick man, and spoke up:

"Your blessing, father! I love the lass more than my life. The woods and I are old friends, and I will not let her come to harm."

Saying this he looked out of his falcon eyes at the girl, but she sank down at the old man's feet.

"Do not force me, Daddy, I must remain faithful to him I promised."

"You will never be his, because I shall kill him. You must be mine or nobody's," replied Black Orlik. "They all will perish here and you will perish also unless I save you."

Black Orlik was right. The utter destruction of the settlement was merely a question of time. They had already begun to slay the cattle bought for tilling the soil. Fever became more frequent; people either cursed or cried out to heaven in a loud voice. One Sun-

day all the men, women and children
knelt down together and there rose a
chorus of mourful voices:

"O Lord, have mercy upon us! O
Lord, save and deliver us from evil."

The voices often broken by sobs rose
to the canopy of heaven and the forest
murmured and rustled "I am King here,
I am Master, I am the stronger."

But Orlik, who knew the woods, looked up with gleaming eyes as if measur-
ing his strength with that impenetrable
wall, and then said aloud:

"We will have a hand to hand tussle
by and by."

The men looked at Orlik with astonishment. Those who had known him
in Texas believed in him implicitly, because he was a great hunter, famous
even among the Texas hunters. He
was powerfully built and would engage
a grizzly single handed. At Saint Antonio, where he had formerly lived,

they knew that when he took his rifle, he might often disappear for months together, but always came back unharmed and in excellent condition. They called him Black Orlik from his tanned complexion. Some said that at a time he was one of a band of pirates but that was not true. He brought skins from the woods, sometimes Indian scalps, until the priest threatened him with excommunication. Now he was almost the only one in Borovina who did not care what happened. He was not troubled about the future. The woods gave him food, shelter, and clothing. When the people began to desert the place he took things into his own hands and in this he was backed up by the lads from Texas. When after the public prayers he was challenging the forest, people thought he must have a new scheme in hand and began to grow less despondent.

The sun had set. High up, between
the branches of the dark hickory trees
gleamed a yellow light which gradually
changed into red and then disappeared.
There was a strong wind blowing from
the South, when at dusk Orlik seized
his rifle and went into the woods.

The night was very dark when the
people in the camp saw something like a
great shining star rising in the distance
above the forest; then appeared a second, a third, which increased in volume,
spreading all round a red, glaring light.

"The forest is on fire! the forest is on
fire!" shouted the terrified spectators.

Great flocks of birds rose screaming
and chattering from the thickets. The
cattle began lowing mournfully, the
dogs howled, and people panic stricken
rushed aimlessly about in fear less the
flames might reach the camp. The conflagration spread rapidly, the flames
diffused themselves like water running

along the dead creepers. The wind tore
off the burning leaves and carried them
along like so many fiery birds.

The hickory trees exploded with a
report like cannons. Like fiery serpents the flames writhed and twisted
around the resinous undergrowth. The
hissing and roaring of the fire mingled
with the screaming of birds and bellowing of beasts rose into a tumult indescribable. The tall trees like so many
fiery columns swayed to and fro. The
burning creepers torn off from the trees
seemed to stretch out demoniacal arms
sending the fiery element from tree to
tree. The sky was of a dusky red as
if the conflagration had spread into the
heavens above. It was almost as light
as in the daytime. Then all the flames
blended into one huge mass of fire which
like the breath of destruction or the
wrath of God rushed through the forest.

The smoke and heat and smell of

burning wood became almost overpower-
ing.   The people, though not threatened
by immediate danger, were still wildly
rushing about searching and calling for
each other, when suddenly from out of
the burning woods, lit up by falling
sparks, emerged the figure of Black Orlik.   His face was begrimed with smoke
and his eyes looked fierce and exultant.
They surrounded him from all sides, and
he leaning on his rifle he said:

"You will not have to cut trees any
longer.   I have burned the woods. To-
morrow you shall have, each of you, as
much land as you can manage."   Then
approaching Marisha, he whispered:

"You must be mine now, for it was
I who burned the forest. Who is
stronger than I?"

The girl trembled in every limb because the wild elements seemed to be
reflected in Orlik's eyes and he was terrible to look at.

For the first time since she had set
foot on American soil, she thanked God
that her Jan was far away in the quiet
Lipincé village.

The roaring fiery waves rushed on
their mad career further and further
away from the camp; at daybreak the
sky was overcast and threatened rain.
The few people who ventured into the
neighborhood of the smouldering woods
were driven back by the intense heat.
The whole day a heavy fog hung in the
air and shrouded the whole landscape
from view. At night, rain began to
fall, which presently changed into a
heavy downpour. Maybe the conflagration shaking the atmosphere contrib-
uted to the breaking of the clouds, or
perhaps it was the time when heavy
rains fell in these regions of big rivers,
swamps, and lakes. The whole encamp-
ment grew soft and muddy and looked
like a vast marsh. The people exposed

to continual wet began to sicken.   More
of the people left the settlement for
Clarksville, but returned soon after with
the terrible news that the river had risen
and their retreat was cut off.

Consternation prevailed in the camp,
provisions were short, and now they
could get nothing from Clarksville.

Laurence and Marisha were less exposed to hunger than the others because
Orlik's strong hand protected them.
Every morning he brought some game
which he either shot or caught in snares.
He had put his own tent over their cabin
wall to protect Marisha and the old man
from rain and wind.   Marisha was obliged to accept all his gifts and be grate-
ful to him, he would take nothing in
return but that which Marisha would
not give him; her love.

"There are other girls in the world,"
she said, " go and choose one among

8

them.   You know my heart belongs to another."

"If I were to search the whole world over, I would not find one like you. You are the only one for me and you must be mine. What will you do if the old man dies? You will come to me of your own accord and I shall carry you off into the forest as the wolf carries a lambkin; but not to devour you. Whom do I fear? Let him come here, that lover of yours, and we shall see who is the stronger man."

When Orlik spoke about the old man dying he judged by what he saw. Laurence was rapidly growing worse; sometimes delirious, and always bemoaning his fate that the Lord was punishing him for his sins and that never again would he behold his native village. Orlik promised and vowed to take Marisha back to Lipincé, but this added more bitterness to the

girl's sorrow.   To go back to the village
where Jan lived as the wife of another
—no! it were better to remain here and
die in the wilderness.   She thought that
would be her fate.

A new disaster was in store for the
settlers.   One night when Orlik was ab-
sent on one of his hunting expeditions,
a great cry was heard in the encamp-
ment: "The water! the water!"

The startled settlers rubbed their eyes,
looked round and saw as far as the eye
could reach a greyish-white expanse
bubbling with heavy raindrops, and a
watery cloud-obscured moon threw her
steely light on the rippling water. From
the woods where the half charred stumps
were dimly visible came the sound of
rushing waves a great tumult arose
The women and children climbed on the
wagons; the men were rushing into the
direction opposite where the trees had
not been cut down.   The water barely

reached their knees but was rising rapidly. The sound of rushing waters
grew louder, and mingled with the cries
of terror and entreaties for help. Presently the animals began to retreat from
place to place, driven by the pressure
of the water. The sheep with plaintive
bleating seemed to ask for help till they
disappeared carried away by the current.
It rained in torrents and soon the distant rushing of the waters changed into
the roar of the unfettered elements.
The wagons began to sway and totter
under the pressure. It soon became
evident that this was not an ordinary
flood caused by heavy rainfall but an
overflow from the Arkansas and its trib-
utaries. The trees snapped like reeds
or were torn out by the roots, the elements seemed to be unchained carrying
with them darkness and death.

One of the wagons standing nearest
the woods toppled over. At the heart-

rending cries of the women, the dark
figures of several men were seen leap-
ing from the trees, but the waves carried the would-be rescuers into the forest to perish.   In other wagons people
clung to the canvass roofs.   The rain
came down unceasingly and still greater
darkness fell on the dusky lake.

Sometimes a log with a human being
clinging to it was bobbing up and down
along the current; sometimes the dark
form of an animal or a man, sometimes
a hand was stretched out of the water
and then disappeared forever.

The bellowing of the beasts and the
agonizing cries and prayers of human
beings were drowned alike in the mighty
roaring of the waters.   Whirlpools and
eddies were forming on the grassy plain,
the wagons were fast disappearing.

And Laurence and Marisha, what had
become of them?   The timbered wall
on which Laurence was lying covered

by Orlik's tent had saved them for the moment, as it floated on the water like a raft. The eddies turned it round and round, and the current carried it towards the woods and bumping against one tree and another pushed it into the bed of the stream and further out into the darkness.

Marisha kneeling by her father's couch, raised her hands to Heaven, calling for help from above; but her only answer was the splashing of the water against the wooden raft.

The tent had been carried off by the wind, and the few planks their only refuge might be dashed to pieces any moment.

Presently it stuck fast between the branches of a tree, the top of which rose above the water At the same minute a human voice called out to them:

"Take my rifle and move to the further side of the raft to keep in it balance. I am going to jump down."

As soon as Laurence and Marisha had obeyed these instructions a dark figure jumped from the branches on to the raft.

It was Orlik.

"Marisha," he said, "as I promised, so I will stand by thee; and may God deal with me as I deal by you."

He took the axe hanging at his side, cut off a stout branch, fashioned it quickly to suit his purpose, pushed the raft out of the tree, and began to row.

Once in the bed of the stream, the current increased their speed and they floated on and on; where they went they did not know.

From time to time Orlik turned the raft aside in order to avoid trees, or pushed stumps or branches out of the way. His strength seemed to increase with every difficulty and his eyes, in spite of the darkness, noticed everything that might endanger their fragile craft. Hour after hour passed. Any ordinary man would have succumbed under the strain; but he did not show any sign of fatigue. Near daybreak they came out of the forest; not a single tree was visible in the distance. The whole country looked like one vast sea. Hideous, foaming waves rolled and whirled over the plain. It became lighter, and Orlik seeing that no immediate danger was to be apprehended stopped rowing for a moment, and turning to Marisha, he said:

"You are mine now, because I snatched you from the jaws of death."

His head was bare, and his face wet and glowing from the single-handed fight with the elements, had such an expression of power and masterfulness, that for the first time Marisha dared not reply that she belonged to another.

"Marisha," said the lad softly, "Marisha. dearest."

"Where are we going?" she asked, endeavoring to change the subject.

"What do I care, as long as we are together, sweetheart."

"Go on rowing, because death is still around us."

Orlik began to row vigorously. Laurence in the meanwhile had grown worse and worse. Sometimes he was delirious, sometimes conscious, but he grew weaker every minute. It was too great a shock, and too much suffering for his old wornout body. He was drawing fast towards the last stage of his wanderings. At noon he woke up and said:

"Marisha! I shall not see the dawn of another day. Oh, child! child! why did I leave my home and drag thee with me into misery? But God is merciful; I have suffered much, and He will forgive my sins. Bury me if you can and let Orlik take thee to New York. The

good gentleman will take care of thee,
and send thee back to Lipincé. I shall
not see it any more. Oh, God! merciful and just, let my soul take wings,
and see the old home once again."

The fever again increased and he began to pray aloud; and then called out in
a terrified voice: "Do not throw me into
the water as if I were a dog." He
seemed suddenly to remember how he
had tried to drown Marisha so as to put
her out of her misery, and cried out
in piteous tones: "Child, forgive! forgive!"

The poor girl was seated at his side,
sobbing pitifully; and Orlik took the
oar with a firmer grasp while tears
gripped him by the throat.

Towards evening it cleared up. The
sun burst out and threw a flood of light
on the watery desert. The old man was
dying, but God was good to him and
gave him an easy end. First he repeated

in mournful tones, over and over
again:

"Why did I leave my own country
and my own village?" by degrees the
feeble voice grew more cheerful. He
was on his way home. The gentleman
at New York had given him money to
buy his little homestead back again and
they are both on their way home. They
are on the ocean; the ship goes night
and day, and the sailors are singing.
Then he sees the harbor whence he em-
barked, towns fly past him, he
hears the sounds of German speech, the
train goes faster and faster and he is
getting nearer home. Joy is expanding
his breast, how different the air feels,
how sweet and refreshing. What is
this—the frontier? The peasant's simple heart beats like a sledge hammer.
Go on! go on! Good God, there are
the fields! that is Malick's pear tree,
the grey cabins, and the church. There
is a peasant in his square cap ploughing

the field.   He stretches his hands out
to him in greeting.   There is the last
station and then comes Lipincé.   Both
he and Marisha are going along the road
weeping.   It is spring, the wheat is in
bloom, and the cockchafers are buzzing
in the air.   They are ringing the bell
for the Angelus.   O Lord Jesus, it is
too much happiness for a sinful man.
One hill to climb and there is the village cross and the boundary of Lipincé.
The peasant throws himself on the
ground and cries like a child, he crawls
up to the cross and hugs it with both
arms; he is home again.

Yes, he is at home; because only the
soulless body remains on the raft in the
midst of the surging flood, and his spirit
has gone where is peace and happiness.
In vain are the sobs and cries of his
daughter: "Daddy, dear, Daddy!" Poor
Marisha, he will not return to thee! He
is too happy in his new home!

The night had come. The improvised oar almost dropped from Orlik's blistered hands and hunger had begun to torment them. Marisha, kneeling near her father's body, was praying; and all around nothing was to be seen but the water. Had they entered into another river? because the current was carrying them along very fast or maybe they were on the prairie as the whirlpools and eddies caused by the hollows were often turning the raft round and round and it was almost impossible to steer it. Orlik felt himself growing fainter, when suddenly, he stood straight up and shouted excitedly:

"By the wounds of Christ! there is a light." Marisha looked in the direction where his arm pointed, and saw a feeble light with its ray reflected in the water.

"It is the boat from Clarksville," said Orlik quickly, "It has been sent out by

the town to save lives. If they could
only see us! Marisha! cheer up, help
is at hand," and he called out with all
his might "Hoop! halloa!" rowing at
the same time with redoubled vigor.

The light gradually increased and by
its red glow they could distinctly see
the outline of a large boat. They were
still far away from it, but the distance
seemed to lessen.

"Is my eyesight failing," muttered
Orlik, after he had rowed some time,
or does the light appear smaller. Yes,
it was growing smaller and dimmer;
they had evidently drifted into another
current.

Suddenly the oar broke in Orlik's
powerful hands and the current carried
them swiftly further away from the
light. Fortunately the raft stuck fast
in the branches of a lonely tree. Both
shouted for help but the rushing water
drowned their voices.

"I am going to fire," said Orlik.
"They will see the flash and hear the
report."

As soon as he said this he raised his
rifle but instead of a flash and crack there
was only the click of the hammer. The
powder was wet.

Orlik threw himself down on the raft,
and remained there like one bereft of
his senses. Presently he raised himself.
"Marisha," he said, in a half dreamy
voice: "I think you have fairly be-
witched me; if you were like other girls
I should have carried you off by force
long ago; there was a time when I
thought of it, but dared not do it for
I loved you. Like a wolf I roamed
solitary in the forest and people were
afraid of me, and now I am timid in
the presence of a girl. I will save you
yet or perish in the attempt. If you
cannot love me it were better you
should be free from me. Marisha, my
love, my sunlight, farewell!"

Before she realized what he was going
to do he had jumped from the raft into
the whirling storm.   For a moment
she saw his dark head emerging from
the water and his arms striking out.
Then he disappeared from view.   He
was swimming towards the boat to summon help.   The fierce current impeded
his motions and dragged him back.   If
he could have got into smoother water
he might have done it, for he was an
expert swimmer, but in spite of superhuman effort he made little progress.
The yellow foaming water blinded his
eyes, he raised his head and peered
through the darkness to see the light
of the boat.   Sometimes a bigger wave
threw him back, another lifted him up,
his breath came quicker and quicker,
and he felt his knees growing stiff.   He
seemed to hear the voice of Marisha
calling for help, and braced himself for
a fresh effort.   Even now he could have

gone back to the raft, carried by the current, but he did not even think of it, because the lights of the boat seemed to come nearer. The fact was that the boat came into his direction carried by the same current that he was struggling against. A few more strokes and he will reach it.

"Help! Help!" The last cry was half smothered by the water which entered into his throat. A wave passed over him but he arose again. The boat was so close to him that he heard the splashing of the oars. He gathered his strength for another cry. They had evidently heard him, because the strokes of the oars became faster. But Orlik went down again. A hideous whirlpool dragged him under. Once more he appeared on the surface, then one hand is lifted above the water, then the other, presently he disappeared altogether.

"In the meanwhile Marisha on the
10

raft alone with the body of her father
stared half unconsciously at the far off
light.   Then, was it her feverish fancy?
but it seemed to come nearer, bear down
upon her, the huge boat which in the
red light and fast moving oars looked
like an immense beetle.

Marisha utterd piercing cries for help.

"I say, Smith; I'll be hanged if I
didn't hear cries of help a few minutes
ago, and just now I heard them again."

A few moments later strong arms carried Marisha into the boat, but Orlik
was not there.

Two months later Marisha left the
hospital of Little Rock, and with money
provided by charitable people, set out
on her way to New York.

The money was not sufficient and she
had to go part of the way on foot, but
she could now speak a little English,
and sometimes the conductors would
give her a lift.   Many people showed

pity to the pale girl with the large blue eyes who looked more like a shadow than a human being. People were not hard; it was life and its conditions which bore hardly on her. What business had this little Polish wildflower in the American whirlpool? The big wheels of life would crush her frail life as cart wheels pass over the flowers on a meadow.

With weak and trembling hand she pulled the bell of the house in Water street, in New York; in search of help from the good old gentleman who hailed from Posen like herself. A stranger opened the door:

"Is Mister Ilotopvlski at home?"

"Who's he?"

"A gentleman, well on in years," here she produced the card.

"He is dead."

"Dead? and his son, Master William?"

"Gone away."

"And Miss Jenny?"

"Gone away."

The door was shut in her face. She sat down on the threshold and wiped her eyes. Here she was again in New York, alone without protection or money, depending on God alone.

What is she to do now? Stay at New York? No, never. She would go to the docks and beg the captains to take her back to Hamburg. From there, on foot and begging her bread she would go back to Lipincé. Jan was there. If he has forgotten his love, and spurns her she would at least die in the old place.

She went to the docks and humbly begged the German captains to take her on their ships. Some of them might have done so, because with a little better living she would look a comely lass, but the rules were against it, and they bade her to go away.

Marisha spent her nights on the same

pier where they had slept that never to
be forgotten night, she and her father.
Fortunately it was summer, and the
nights were warm.

At daybreak she was always at the
German docks to renew her prayers to
be taken across the Atlantic and always
in vain. She grew weaker every day,
and felt that unless she sailed soon, she
would die, as died all those that had
been connected with her fate. But,
with the quiet endurance of the peasant
she still clung to hope.

One morning she crept there thinking
it would be the last time, as her strength
was ebbing fast. She resolved to beg
no more, but get into a ship sailing for
Europe, and hide somewhere quietly.
When, later on, they should find her
they would not throw her into the water;
and if they did, what would it matter?
It was all one to her how she died, if
die she must. But on the gangway

leading to the ship, the man on watch rudely pushed her back. She sat down on some lumber near the water and thought the fever was getting hold of her again. She began to smile strangely and mutter to herself:

"I am a great heiress now, but always faithful. Jan, don't you recognize your Marisha?"

It was not fever but insanity.

Henceforth she came every day to the docks to wait for the ship which was to bring her lover. People came to know her and gave her small gifts. She thanked them humbly and smiled at them like a child. This continued for two months. One morning she did not come and was seen no more.

The newspapers reported the next day that the body of a girl, name and whereabouts unknown, had been found dead on the furthest end of the pier.

AN ARTIST'S END
(*Lux in Tenebris Lucet*)

AN ARTIST'S END.

There are days, especially in November, so dark, damp, and gloomy that even to those endowed with a good constitution, life becomes a thing of utter weariness.

Ever since Kamionka had begun to feel ill and left off working at his statue of charity this same weather had oppressed him more than his physical ailment. Morning after morning he rose from his couch, wiped the large studio window and peered anxiously out to see whether there was any change in the weather; but the same dreary vista met his eyes. A leaden mist shrouded the earth; it did not rain, yet the flags in the court yard were covered with a greasy moisture, everything was soaked

with wet, and the large drops falling
from the waterspout seemed to beat time
to the slowly dragging hours of sadness.

The window of the studio looked upon
the yard and garden beyond. The grass
across the railings still looked green with
the sickly greenness of death and decay;
the trees were stripped of all but a few
yellow leaves and the black, dripping
branches seen dimly through the mist
presented a ghost-like appearance. The
rooks which had chosen them for their
winter quarters flapped their wings and
cawed loudly before settling down among
the branches.

On days like these the studio looked
like a mortuary. Marble and plaster of
Paris require light and sunny skies. In
the dim light their whiteness looked
mournful, and the darker terra albas
losing all distinctness of outline, took
indescribable, almost hideous shapes.
Dirt and untidiness added not a little to

the desolation of the place. Dust mixed
with bits of clay, and dirt carried in from
the street covered the floor. The walls,
discolored by age, were bare except for a
few casts of hands and feet; not far
from the window hung a small looking-
glass surmounted by a horse's skull, and
a bunch of withered flowers.

In one corner stood the bed covered
with an old, crumpled counterpane, near
it a little table with an iron candlestick.
Kamionka, to save expense, lived and
slept in the studio. The bed was usually
concealed by a screen; but now the
screen had been removed so that the sick
man might be able to watch the window opposite for the sun to come out.
There was another still larger window in
the roof, but this was so encrusted with
dust and dirt that even on bright days
it emitted but a scanty light.

It did not clear up. After several days
of gloominess the clouds sunk lower yet;

the air became more and more saturated
with mist and it grew darker still. The
artist who had lain down on his bed fully
dressed began to feel worse; he took off
his clothes and got up no more.

He did not suffer from any particular
disease; he only felt very tired, very sad,
and a general weakness seemed to numb
his limbs. He did not wish for death,
yet could not summon energy enough to
live.

The long hours of darkness seemed to
him all the longer, as he had nobody near
him. His wife had died twenty years
before; his relations lived in another part
of the country and he had no friends.
His acquaintances had gradually deserted him because of his increasing ill tem-
per. At the beginning people had
smiled at his cantankerous humors, but
when he became more and more of an
oddity and took offence at the slightest
joke, even those that knew him best
broke off all intercourse.

They also resented that he had grown
pious with advancing years and doubted
his sincerity.   Malicious tongues whispered that he went to church in order to
get commissions from the priests. They
were wrong. His piety was not, perhaps,
the outcome of a firm and deep-rooted
conviction, but it was genuine. The only
thing said against him founded upon
truth was his ever increasing miserliness.
For many years he had lived in his studio
upon the scantiest of fares, which undermined his constitution and gave his face
the waxlike hue.

He avoided people, fearing they might
want something from him. His was a
warped nature, embittered and very unhappy. But for all this his character was
not a common one, as even his faults had
an artistic stamp. Those who fancied he
hoarded money were wrong. Kamionka
was a poor man because he spent all his
money upon etchings, of which he had a

large collection. He looked at them now
and then and counted them with the
greed of a miser gloating over his gold.
He kept this a secret from everybody,
perhaps for the very reason that the fancy had sprung from a great sorrow and
deep feelings.

A year or two after the death of his
wife he had come across an old etching,
the center figure of which recalled to
him the features of his dead wife.   He
bought the print and ever afterwards
looked about to find the same likeness in
others and gradually, as the fancy got
hold of him, he bought anything in the
same line that pleased his artistic eye.

People who have lost what they held
most precious in life are obliged to fill
up the void, otherwise they could not ex-
ist. As to Kamionka nobody would have
thought that this elderly egoist had once
loved a woman more than his life.   Had
she not died, his life most likely would

have been different, more peaceful, and
human. As it was this love had outlived
his talent, youth and happier times.

The piety which gradually became a
regular custom, based upon the observa-
tion of outward forms, had sprung from
the same source. Kamionka was not one
of those who clung to religious beliefs;
he began to pray after the death of his
wife because it seemed to him that this
was the only thing now he could do for
her, the only link which connected him
with her. Natures apparently cold and
impassive are often endowed with an in-
tensity of feeling little suspected by their
surroundings. After the death of his
wife all Kamionka's thoughts twined
around her memory and drew nourishment from it like the parasite plant from
the tree to which it clings; but the human mind cannot subsist on this kind of
nutriment; it distorts it and throws it off
its balance.

Had he not been an artist he could not
have survived his loss: his art saved him.
It is useless to tell the survivor that it
matters nothing to the dead in what
grave they rest.   Kamionka wished his
dead wife to have the best he could give
her and he worked at her monument as
much with his heart as hands.   This
saved him from madness and prevented
his giving way altogether.

The man remained warped and unhappy, but art had saved the artist.
Henceforth Kamionka lived only for his
art.

Very few in looking at pictures or
sculptures give any thought as to whether the artist has treated his subject hon-
estly or otherwise. Upon this point Kamionka was without reproach.   He was not
a genius, and his gift only a little above
the average, therefore it could not fill his
whole life or compensate him for his loss,
but such as it was he respected it deeply

and was always true to it. During all his
life he never insulted or wronged his art,
either for fame, lucre, or blame.   He
created what he felt. In those happy
times when he lived like other men he
used to speak about art in quite an un-
common way and when afterwards people began to avoid him he thought of it
in the loneliness of his studio with the
same reverence and honesty.

Human beings in relation to each
other have certain unwritten laws in vir-
tue of which the exceptionally unhappy
ones are condemned to solitude It is the
stone thrust out of the riverbed, ceasing
to rub against other stones, becomes in-
crusted with moss, so the human unit
separated from his fellows acquires faults
and oddities.

Now when Kamionka lay ill nobody
came to see him except the charwoman,
who looked in twice a day to fill his
samovar and prepare the tea.   She ad-

11

vised to send for the doctor, but he scout-
ed the idea, being afraid of the expense.

At last he grew very faint, perhaps
because he took no nourishment except
tea. But he had no desire for anything,
either to eat or to work, or to live. His
thoughts were as limp as the autumn
leaves he saw through the window, and
in harmony with the mist and darkness
outside. There are no worse moments in
human eixstence than when it is brought
home to us that all has been done there
was to do, and that life can give us nothing more. Kamionka for nearly fifteen
years had lived in continual terror lest
his talent should give out. Now he was
sure of it and he thought with bitterness
that even his art had deserted him. He
felt weary and utterly exhausted. He
did not expect to die soon, but did not
believe he could get better.

Altogether there was not a spark of
hope in him.

If he wished for anything it were for the sun to come out and shine through the window. He thought that might revive him a little. He had always been sensitive to the changes of weather, and rain or darkness always influenced his spirit, and now this hopeless weather, as he called it, had come when he lay prostrated on his bed.

Every morning when the woman came with his tea Kamionka asked:

"How does it look outside? Do you think it is clearing up?"

"Ah, no," answered the woman, "there is such a mist that one cannot see anybody within a yard."

The sick man hearing this shut his eyes wearily and remained motionless for hours.

In the courtyard everything was silent but for the slow continual drip of the waterspout. .

At three o'clock in the afternoon it

grew so dark that Kamionka had to light
the candle. This, being so weak, cost
him no little trouble. Before stetching
out his hand for the matches he thought
it over, then raised his arm, the thinness
of which showing through the night
dress offended his artistic taste; after he
had lit the candle, he fell back again,
and remained motionless, listening with
closed eyes to the monotonous drip of the
water, until the charwoman came in for
the second time.

The studio presented a strange sight.
The flame of the candle lit up the bed
and the artist lying upon it, and concentrated itself in one luminous point on the
forehead, which looked like old polished
ivory. The remainder of the room lay
in deep shadow, which increased and
thickened gradually. But in proportion
as the darkness increased the statues
seemed to grow more lifelike. The flame
of the candle rose and fell, and in the

flickering lights they too seemed to move
and stand on tip-toe to look at the
emaciated frame of the sculptor, curious
to know whether their creator were still
among the living.

And truly there was in that face a
certain rigidity of death. But from time
to time the pale lips moved as if in
prayer, or maybe silently complained of
his loneliness, and the everlasting drip
from the waterspout, which always with
the same precision, seemed to measure
the time of his illness.

One evening the charwoman came in
smelling strongly of alcohol, therefore
more than usually loquacious, and said:

"There is so much work on my hands
that I can only just manage to look in
twice a day. Why not send for a sister
of mercy? They do not cost anything,
and it would be more comfortable for
you."

The idea pleased Kamionka, but like

most queer tempered people, he liked to
oppose what anybody advised him, he
therefore refused.

After the woman had gone he began
to turn it over in his mind. A sister of
mercy! It was true they did not take
money and what help and comfort she
would have been to him! Kamionka,
like other sick people left to themselves,
had to bear various discomforts and
small miseries which hurt him as much
as they irritated him. Sometimes his
head was lying in an uncomfortable position for hours and he could not summon
energy enough to rearrange the pillows;
then at nights he often felt chilly and
would have given anything for some hot
tea, but if the lighting of the candle
caused him difficulty how could he think
of boiling the water? A sister of mercy
would do all that for him with the ut-
most cheerfulness. How much easier it
would be to bear illness with somebody
to help him.

The poor man worked himself up to that extent that it appeared to him even illness under such conditions were something almost desirable and wondered inwardly that all this lay within his reach.

The thought also that if the sister came the studio would look more cheerful, even the clouds might lift and the unceasing drip of the waterspout cease to haunt him.

Then he began to regret that he had not agreed at once to the woman's proposal. The long, gloomy night was before him and he could not see her till next morning. It dawned upon him that this night of all others would be the longest and the heaviest to bear.

Thoughts flitted through his brain of what an utter outcast he was and he began to compare his former life with what it now was. And as the thought of the sister, so now the days past and gone, seemed to be closely allied with sunshine and bright skies.

He began thinking of his dead wife and to pour out all his grief and sorrow to her as he always did when he felt very miserable. At last he grew tired and fell asleep.

The candle on the little table burned down. The flame changed from pink into a bluish hue, then flickered up once and twice and went out. The studio was now wrapped up in utter darkness.

In the meantime outdoors the drops of water fell one by one as if all the sadness and gloom were filtering slowly through nature's bosom.

Kamionka slept long and peacefully, when suddenly he woke up under the impression that something unusual was taking place in the studio. It was towards daybreak. The marble statues and plaster of paris casts began to whiten. A pale light shone through the window opposite. By this light Kamionka saw somebody sitting near his bed.

He opened his eyes very wide and
looked. It was a sister of mercy.

She sat quite motionless, a little
turned towards the window, with her
head bent down. Her hands were crossed
on her knees—she seemed to pray. The
sick man could not see her face, but he
saw distinctly the white coif and the
dark outline of the somewhat thin
shoulders.

His heart began to beat a little anxiously and the question rose in his mind:

"When could the charwoman have
fetched the sister, and how did she come
in?"

Presently he thought it must be the
fancy of a weakened brain and he shut
his eyes. After a few moments he
opened them again.

The sister was still sitting in the same
place, motionless as if absorbed in prayers.

A strange feeling, partly of joy and

partly of fear made his hair rise. Something incomprehensible seemed to draw him towards that silent figure. He fancied to have seen her before—but where and when he could not remember. He felt a great longing to see the face hidden under the white coif. Kamionka, without understanding it himself, dared neither move or speak; he scarcely dared to breathe. He only felt that fear and joy possessed his whole being and asked himself wonderingly: What does it mean?

It had grown quite light now. What a wonderful morning it must be outdoors he thought. Suddenly, without any transition, a great flood of light came in through the window, a light as strong and radiant as comes in the month of May. Waves of golden sunshine seemed to pour in and fill the room, the statues and marbles disappeared within, the very walls seemed absorbed by it—and Ka-

mionka found himself in a lighted end-
less space.

He looked at the sister, the white coif,
which concealed her features, seemed to
shake with a sudden tremor, and the
glorious light touched the bent head.

She turned it slowly towards the sick
man and suddenly the deserted outcast
saw as in a glory the well-known features
of his beloved wife.

He rose from his bed, and from his
breast came a cry, which spoke of years
of bitterness, tears, and sorrow:

"Lozia! Lozia!"

And taking hold of her he pressed her
to his heart and she threw both arms
around his neck.

The light grew stronger and stronger.

"You remained true to me," she said
at last, "therefore I came and prayed
that death might deal gently by you."

Kamionka was still holding her in his
arms for fear the holy vision might dis-

appear together with the light. "I am ready to die," he said, "if only I could keep you with me."

A smile of exceeding sweetness lit up her face and taking one hand from around his neck she pointed down and said:

"You are dead; look there!"

Kamionka's eyes followed the direction of her hand and there below, under his feet, he looked through the skylight into the dim lonely studio; there on the bed lay his body, the wide-open mouth forming a decavity on the yellow waxen face. He looked upon the emaciated form as upon a strange thing. He soon lost sight of it altogether, because the wave of light, as if moved by a breeze from other worlds, carried them higher and higher into space.

A COMEDY OF ERRORS
A Sketch of American Life

A COMEDY OF ERRORS.

Five or six years ago it happened that oil was discovered somewhere in the county of Mariposa, in California. The enormous profits derived from oil in Nevada and other states, speedily brought speculators to the spot, who formed a company and brought out pumps, barrels of all sizes and dimensions, and all the machinery necessary for sinking wells. Some fifty houses were erected for the workmen, the place named "Struck Oil," and shortly, as if by magic, a settlement sprung into life where formerly had been a barren wilderness, inhabited only by coyotes.

Two years later Struck Oil became a city, and was a city in the full meaning of the word. Please to note: There was already a shoemaker, a tailor, a carpenter, a blacksmith, a butcher, and a doctor. The latter a Frenchman, who in bygone times had shaved beards in France, but nevertheless had some surgical knowledge and was harmless, which in an American doctor means a great deal.

The doctors, as is often the case in a small town, had an apothecary's shop. He was also postmaster, and had, therefore, three strings to his bow.

As an apothecary he was equally harmless, as his whole stock consisted in colored syrups and Leroy. This quiet and gentle old man would say to his patients:

"Do not be afraid of my physic. I take a dose myself every time I prescribe to a patient, and if it does not hurt a healthy man, it is sure not to harm a sick one. Now don't you think so?"

"That's true," replied the satisfied patients. It never occurred to them that it was the doctor's duty not only not to injure a patient, but to help him.

Monsieur Dasonville, that was the doctor's name, was a staunch believer in the marvellous effects of leroy. Frequently at public meetings he would bare his head and turn to his audience with these words:

"Ladies and gentlemen, you see in me the happy effects of leroy. I am seventy years old, and during forty years of my life, I have never failed to take a daily dose, and behold, I have not a single grey hair on my head."

He had no grey hair, that was true enough; but then it might have been remarked that he had none at all, as his head was as smooth as a billiard ball; but as this had nothing whatever to do with the development of the city, the doctor's speech remained unchallenged.

In the meanwhile Struck Oil City grew larger and larger. Presently a

12

railway branch was established to connect the city with the world in general; and its officials decided upon. The doctor as a representative of learning, a man universally liked and respected, was chosen as judge; the shoemaker, Mr. Davis, a Polish Jew, became the head of the police force, which consisted of the sheriff and nobody else; a school was built, and its management entrusted to a schoolma'am, specially imported, an ancient spinster with a chronic faceache; and last, but not least, there rose the first hotel under the name of the United States Hotel.

Business flourished. The exportation of oil brought immense profits.

Mr. Davis erected a bay-window before his shop in imitation of those in 'Frisco.' At the next meeting the citizens offered him a vote of thanks for having embellished the city; upon which the sheriff, with the proud humility of a great man, said:

"Thank you! oh, thank you!"

Where there is a judge and a sheriff there are likely to be lawsuits. This called for writing material; therefore, at the corner of Coyote and First streets a stationer established himself, who sold also newspapers and political caricatures, representing General Grant as a boy milking a cow: the United States. It was not the sheriff's duty to prohibit the sale of caricatures, as the police had nothing to do with that.

What would an American town be without a newspaper? At the end of the second year a paper under the title of the "Saturday Weekly Review," made its appearance and had as many subscribers as there were people in the city. The editor of the paper was at the same time sub-editor, printer and distributor. The last duty did not cause him any inconvenience, as he kept a dairy and personally supplied the citizens with milk.

These humble duties did not prevent him
from beginning his political articles
something after this fashion: "If our
benighted President had followed the advice given him in our last issue," etc.,
etc.

It is seen, therefore, that not a single
blessing was lacking in Struck Oil City.
The sheriff's duties were not heavy, as
the miners working the oil-wells had
none of the violent and rowdy spirit of
the gold-diggers; and things were generally pretty quiet. Nobody fought anybody, lynch-law was unknown, and the
days flowed peacefully, one exactly like
the other. The first half of the day was
devoted to business, and in the evening
when there were no meetings, the citizens burnt rubbish in the street, and
then went to bed; in the blissful consciousness that they would do the same
thing the day following.

The sheriff's only trouble was that he

could not prevail upon the citizens not to fire at the wild geese which at sunset were seen flying over the city. The law prohibits using firearms in public thoroughfares. "If it were a scurvy little town," remarked the sheriff, "I wouldn't say anything against the practice, but in a respectable city to go on bang! banging in the streets, is, to say the least, unbecoming."

The citizens listened deferentially to his speech, nodded their heads, and said: "Yes, yes," but when the evening came and on the rosy sky appeared the long grey line of the birds flying towards the ocean, everybody forgot his promise, grasped the rifle, and the shooting began as merrily as ever.

Mr. Davis might have brought the culprits before the judge to be fined heavily, but we must not forget that the offenders were the judge's patients in case of sickness, and which happened oftener,

the sheriff's customers when their boots
wore out, and as one hand washes the
other, it is not likely one hand would
hurt the other.   Peace and quietness
reigned therefore in Struck Oil City,
when suddenly that delightful state of
things came to an end.

Two storekeepers had risen against
each other in mortal feud.   In the stores
was everything which mortal man or
woman can want or desire: hats, cigars,
paper-collars, shirts, blouses, and all
sorts of groceries.   In the beginning
there was but one store, kept by Hans
Kasche, a phlegmatic German from
Prussia.   He was about thirty-five years
old, not exactly fat, but round and comfortable looking.   He always walked
about in his shirt sleeves and never part-
ed company with his pipe.   He knew
enough English for his business, and no
more; but to the latter he attended so
diligently, that after a year it was said

by those who knew that he was worth several thousand dollars.

Suddenly a second store made its appearance opposite Hans Kasche.

By a singular chance the rival establishment was also kept by a German, a Miss Neuman, or, as she styled herself, Newman. The two dealers looked askance at each other from the beginning, but open hostilities did not break out until Miss Neuman gave an "Opening" luncheon, and the cakes there served were found to be baked from flour adulterated with soda and alum. She would have compromised herself in public opinion had she not declared that the flour had been purchased at Hans Kasche's; her own not being yet unpacked. It became evident that Hans must be a rascal, who, devoured by envy, had tried to ruin his rival at the very outset. Everybody anticipated skirmishes between the two, but did not foresee that so much personal animosity would be mixed up with it. It was commented upon by the citizens that Hans never burned his rubbish, but when the wind blew in the direction of his rival's store. Miss Neuman never spoke of Hans but as the "Dutchman," which gave mortal offence.

In the beginning the citizens made fun of both parties, especially as neither of them spoke English; but gradually, from their daily relations with the grocers two parties began to form themselves in the city, the Neumanites and the Hansimists, who looked askance at each other, which undermined the general harmony and threatened the city with dire complications. The diplomatic sheriff tried in vain to stem the torrent at its source and to conciliate the two Germans. He was often seen standing in the middle of the street addressing them in their native tongue:

"Come now, why should you quarrel?

Don't you buy your boots in the same establishment? I have got just now such a lovely assortment, none better to be found in San Francisco."

"What is the use of recommending your boots to people who will have to do without them before long?" interrupted the lady, acrimoniously.

"I do not attract customers by my feet," replied phlegmatic Hans.

Now Miss Neuman, though a German, had beautiful feet, and this covert sneer filled her with wrath unspeakable.

At the meetings, the affairs of the two rival dealers begin to evoke discussion and, as in America, in the case of a woman, justice is doubly blindfolded, therefore the majority leaned towards Miss Neuman.

Presently Hans became aware that his customers began to fall off. Miss Neuman likewise thought her business did not go on as well as it ought to. The

fact was all the women stood by Hans.
They remarked that their husbands fre-
quented the lady's store too much and
lingered too long over their purchases.

When no customers were to be served
in either store, Hans and Miss Neuman
stood in their doors casting at each other
looks of scorn and hatred. Miss Neuman often sung a ditty to the tune of
"Mein lieber Augustin."

"Dutchman! Dutchman, oh Du-Du-
Dutchman!"

Hans looked at her feet, then at her
figure, his eyes slowly travelling up-
wards to her face with an expression as
if he were examining a dead coyote;
then burst into demoniacal laughter,
saying:

"Mein Gott!"

The hatred in this phlegmatic man
had now developed to such an extent
that when he stood before his door and
did not see his rival he felt uncomfortable.

More overt hostilities would have broken out before this had not Hans been sure that he would get the worst of any public exposure, as Miss Neuman had the editor of the "Weekly Review" on her side. He had become aware of this after he had circulated the news that Miss Neuman had a made up figure. A slashing article appeared in the paper pointing out the slandering propensities of the Germans in general, and wound up with an assurance that being well-informed he considered it his duty to inform his readers that the figure of a certain calumniated lady was nature's handiwork.

From this day forth Hans took his coffee without milk, whereas Miss Neuman took double the amount. She also had herself measured for a tailor-made dress, which decisively convinced everybody that Hans was a slanderer.

In presence of female cunning Hans

felt himself at his wits end, and there in the open door stood the fair enemy singing her ditty about the "Dutchman."

"What can I do to her?" thought Hans vindictively. "I have some wheat poisoned for rats, if I poisoned her poultry? No, they would make me pay for it. I know what I will do."

In the evening Miss Neuman perceived with astonishment that Hans was carrying armfulls of wild sunflower stalks up to his cellar window. "I should like to know what he is up to now, it's sure to be something against me!"

It had now grown almost dark, but she could still see Hans spreading the stalks in two lines, leaving a little path free towards the cellar window; he then brought something carefully wrapped up in a cloth, he turned his back to where Miss Neuman was watching him, took the cloth from the mysterious object, placed it tenderly on the ground and covered it with dry leaves; then approached the wall and began writing upon it.

Miss Neuman was quivering with excitement.

"He is writing something spiteful against me," she thought. "I shall see what it is as soon as everybody is in bed, if it cost me my life."

When Hans had finished his work he went leisurely into his house and soon afterwards extinguished the light. Then Miss Neuman hastily donned her wrapper, thrust her bare feet into slippers, and went into the street. When she came to the sunflowers, she went straight across the little footpath up to the window in order to see the inscription on the wall. Suddenly her eyes opened wide in terror, the upper part of her body swayed backwards and an agonizing cry burst from her lips:

"Help! help!"

A sash in the upper story was lifted gently.

"Was is das?" said the even voice of Hans. "Was is das?"

"Cursed Dutchman," screamed the lady, "you have killed me, murdered me. To-morrow you will be hung. Help! help!"

"I am coming directly," said Hans.

Presently he appeared with a lighted candle. He looked at Miss Neuman, who seemed rooted to the spot; then he put his arms akimbo, and burst into a shout of merry laughter.

"Ho! ho! ho! It's Miss Neuman! Ho! ho! ho! Good evening, Miss. I set a trap for skunks and caught a young lady. What were you doing at my cellar window? I wrote a warning on the wall to prevent people coming near it. Scream away; let people come and see that you come at nights to look into the Dutchman's cellar window. Oh, mein

Gott! scream as loud as you can, but you will have to remain where you are till morning. Good night, Miss Neuman, good night!"

Miss Neuman's position was dreadful. If she kept on screaming people would collect and see her thus; what a scandal! If she did not scream she would have to stop here all night and be seen by people next morning, and beside her foot was becoming very painful. Her head began to swim, the stars seemed to melt one into the other, the moon showed the fiendish countenance of Herr Hans. She fainted.

"Herr Je!" ejaculated Hans to himself, "suppose she dies? They would lynch me without trial!"

And his hair stood on end with sudden terror. He searched for the key of the trap, but it was not easy to unlock it, as Miss Neuman's wrapper was in the way. He had to push it aside and . . . in spite of his hatred and terror he could not help looking admiringly at the little marble feet, visible now in the reddish light of the moon.

He unlocked the trap quickly, and as the lady gave no sign of returning consciousness he lifted her in his strong arms and carried her across the street into her own house. During the short transit his hatred and aversion seemed to have vanished into space and the only feeling he was conscious of possessing was a gentle pity and compassion for his helpless enemy. He returned to his house, and tossed restlessly on his bed all night. Something had disturbed phlegmatic Hans' equanimity.

The next morning Miss Neuman did not appear in the doorway, and did not sing about the "Dutchman." Maybe she felt ashamed or maybe she was silently plotting her revenge.

The sequel showed that it was the

latter. That same evening the editor of the "Weekly Review" challenged Hans to fight, and began by giving him a black eye. But Hans' blood was up and he began to use his fists so vigorously that the editor was thrown full length on the ground and cried out: "Enough! Enough!"

Nobody knew how it happened, it was not through Hans that the whole town came to know of Miss Neuman's nocturnal adventure. After the fight with the editor, all softer feelings vanished from Hans Kasche's heart, and he hated his rival as cordially as ever.

He had a foreboding that the inimical hand was preparing new blows, and he had not long to wait for it either. Americans use ice largely and Hans always kept a good supply of it in his cellar. Gradually he became aware that nobody applied for ice to him any longer. The huge slabs he had brought by railroad

13

were melting down and he was already some fifteen dollars out of pocket. How was it? He saw his own partisans buying it in the opposite stores. He could not make out what it meant, but resolved to find out the reason. The saloon-keeper, Peters, passed his door.

"Why do you not take your ice from me any longer?" he asked.

"Because you have not got any," replied Peters.

"*Aber*! I keep ice always," said Hans.

"And what's that for?" asked the saloon-keeper, pointing to a notice stuck up on the wall.

Hans looked, and turned green with rage. In the word "Notice" the t had been carefully erased and read "No ice."

"Donnerwetter!" shouted Hans, and with livid face and trembling limbs he rushed into Miss Neuman's store.

"That's a rascally business," he shouted with foaming mouth. "Why did you scratch out that letter, Miss?"

"What did you say I scratched out?" asked Miss Neuman innocently.

"The letter t I say. You scratched out the t, but donnerwetter, this must be ended, you will have to pay me for the ice."

Poor Hans had lost his usual composure and danced and shouted about the place like one bereft of his senses. Miss Neuman began to scream and people rushed into the store.

"Help! help!" she called out. "The Dutchman is gone mad! He says I have scratched something out. What should I scratch out unless it were his eyes, if he goes on like that. I am a poor, lonely woman; he means to kill me, to murder me."

Saying this she broke out in tears. The people did not understand what it was all about; but they could not stand by and see a woman shed tears; they therefore took the German by the scruff of the neck and tried to evict him. Hans resisted valiantly, but in vain; out he had to go, and out he went flying across the street into his own store, where he fell headlong on the ground.

A week later a painted signboard appeared above his store. It represented a monkey dressed in a striped gown, white apron and bib, a dress exactly like that Miss Neuman used to wear. Underneath was the inscription:

"Stores at the sign of the monkey."

People collected before the store. Their merriment brought Miss Neuman into the street. She looked at the signboard and changed color, but with great presence of mind she called out at once:

"A very appropriate sign for Herr Kasche!"

But all the same the blow had struck home. At noon when the children, coming from school, stopped before the picture, she had to listen to their mocking comments:

"Oh, that's Miss Neuman! Good morning, Miss Neuman!"

This was too much. When the editor came with the milk, she said:

"The monkey is meant for me. I know it's me, and I shall never forgive him for the insult. He shall be forced to take it down and lick it off with his tongue in my presence!"

"What do you intend to do about it, Miss?"

"I will go to the judge."

"Now?"

"To-morrow."

The next morning on leaving the store she approached Hans.

"Listen, Herr Dutchman, I know that monkey is meant for me. You come with me to the judge and we will see what he says about it?"

"He will say that anybody has the right to hang out a signboard."

"We'll soon see about that."

Miss Neuman could scarcely breathe.

"And how do you know it was meant for you, Miss?"

"My conscience tells me. Come at once to the judge, unless you wish the sheriff to bring you there in handcuffs."

"Very well, I will go," said Hans, who felt sure the judge could do nothing to him.

They locked their stores and departed —abusing each other heartily on the way.

At the very door of Monsieur Dasonville they remembered that they did not know English sufficiently well to explain the case. No, it wouldn't do, they must first go to the sheriff. The sheriff was sitting on his wagon ready to start off on a journey.

"Go to the devil!" he exclaimed quickly. "You two disturb the whole town, and your boots last you out the whole summer. I am going to fetch lumber. Good bye!"

And off he went at a brisk trot.

Hans put his arms akimbo.

"You will have to wait till to-morrow, Miss," he said, phlegmatically.

"I shall not wait! I would rather die —unless you take down your signboard."

"I will not take it down, Miss."

"Then you will swing for it! You will be hanged, Dutchman."

"We can do without the sheriff. The judge knows all about the matter without our telling him."

Miss Neuman was wrong for once. The judge was the only man in the city who did not know anything about their quarrels. The harmless old man was busy preparing his leroy and fancied he was saving the world.

He received them as he received everybody, kindly and with perfect politeness.

"Show your tongues, my children, I will soon give you a prescription.

Both waved their arms to show it was not for a prescription they had come. Miss Neuman repeated: "It is not that we want."

"What is it then?"

Both talked at once. To Hans's one word Miss Neuman had ten. At last the lady hit upon means to make him understand; she pointed at her heart, to show how wounded it was by Hans Kasche's behavior.

The judge's face brightened. "I understand," he said, "I understand."

Then he opened a book and began to write. He asked Hans his age. "Thirty-six." Then he asked the lady: she did not remember accurately, but thought it was about twenty-five. "All right!"

"What Christian name? Hans-Lora. All right!"

"What occupation?" "Storekeepers." "All right!" Then a few other questions which they did not understand, but answered yes. The judge nodded all was over.

He left off writing, rose, and to the astonishment of Lora took her in his arms and kissed her on both cheeks. She took this for a good omen, and full of pleasant anticipation returned home.

"I will show you now who has got the upper hand," said Miss Neuman.

"You will show some one else then," said the German quietly.

The next morning the sheriff passed near the stores. Both stood at their doors. Hans puffed at his pipe. Miss Neuman was singing.

"Do you wish to go to the judge?" asked the sheriff.

"We have been there."

"Well, what does he say?"

"Dear Sheriff, good Herr Davis, go and ask him what he intends to do; and please say a word for me. You see, I am a poor, lonely girl. I shall visit you soon as I am in want of boots."

The sheriff left, but returned in a
quarter of an hour—and for some in-
explicable reason was surrounded by a
crowd of people.

"Well, what is it?" asked both liti-
gants, eagerly.

"It's all right! It's all right!" said
the sheriff.

"And what has the judge done for
us?"

"What should he have done? He has
married you!"

"Married us?"

"What is there so astonishing in that?
People do marry."

If a thunderbolt had fallen in their
midst they could not have been more
startled. Hans opened his eyes and
mouth and stared stupidly at Miss Neuman, and Miss Neuman stared in blank
amazement at Hans.

"I to be his wife?"

"I to be her husband?"

"Oh horror! never! We must have a divorce at once!"

"I would rather die than live with the man. We must get divorced; oh, what a misfortune!"

"My dears," said the sheriff quietly, "what is the use of all this noise? The judge can marry you, but he cannot divorce you. What is there to cry out about? Are you millionaires to be able to go for a divorce to San Francisco? Do you know what it will cost you? Take it easy. I have beautiful baby shoes, sell 'em you cheap. Good bye!"

Saying this, he went on his way. The people dispersed laughing, and the newly married couple remained alone.

"It's that Frenchman," exclaimed the bride. "He has done it on purpose, knowing we are both Germans."

"*Richtig* (correct)," replied Hans.

"But we will have a divorce."

"I agree with you there, Miss. What

a mean thing it was for you to scratch
that letter out."

"I was not the first to begin; you
caught me in a spring trap."

"I don't care for you, Miss."

"I hate you."

Upon this they separated and shut up
their stores. She remained shut up all
the day, thinking; and he did the same.
Night brings rest and peace. They retired, but could not sleep. He thought:
"There sleeps my wife." She thought:
"There sleeps my husband." And
strange feelings grew up in their hearts.
It was still anger and hatred, but with
them, an overwhelming sensation of
loneliness. Beside that Hans thought of
the sign board over his door. He would
not let it remain now, it was a caricature
of his wife. And it struck him that after
all it had been a mean thing to have had
it painted and hung up there. But then
he hated her; it was through her his ice

thawed; it was true he had caught her in a trap; and he saw again before his eyes the pretty, bare feet, with the moonlight playing upon them. She is a nice enough girl, but she hates me and I do not like her. What a situation. Ach! Herr Gott!" to be married to Miss Neuman. And a divorce costs so much money, that all his savings would be insufficient to cover the expense.

"I am the wife of that Dutchman," said Miss Neuman to herself. "I am no longer a maiden, but a married woman. And to think that I am married to that fellow Kasche who caught me in a springtrap. It's true, he took me in his arms and carried me upstairs. How strong he is. What noise is that?"

There was no noise, but Miss Neuman was frightened, she, who had never been frightened before. "It's very lonely for a single woman; it would be different with a man in the house. Murders had

been committed before on lonely women
(she had not thought of it before), somebody might kill and rob her some day.
And to think that now that man Kasche
has barred me from matrimony. We
must soon get a divorce, there's comfort
in that."

Thinking and thinking she turned
restlessly in her bed.

Suddenly she started, yes there was
a noise, she had not been mistaken. In
the stillness of the night she distinctly
heard the knocking of a hammer.

"Good Lord!" screamed the lady,
"some burglar is trying to get into the
store."

She jumped from her bed, put on her
wrapper and rushed to the window; but
what she saw there completely restored
the balance of her mind. By the light of
the moon she saw a ladder, and perched
on it the comfortable looking Hans, who,
hammer in hand, knocked out one by

one the nails which fastened the signboard over his store.

"It is good-natured on his part, he is
taking down the monkey."

And she felt as if something was melting in her heart.

Now the nails had all been withdrawn
and the plate came rattling to the
ground.   Then he descended, knocked
off the frame, rolled the sheet into a
tube, and then removed the ladder.

The lady followed all his motions with
her eyes.   The night was quiet and
warm.

"Herr Hans!" called she in a low tone.

"You are not asleep, Miss?" whispered
Hans.

"No; good evening, Herr Hans."

"Good evening, Miss."

"What are you doing?"

"I have taken down the monkey."

"Thank you, Herr Hans."

After that there was a slight pause.

"Herr Hans," whispered again the voice from the window.

"What is it, Fräulein Lora?"

"We must consult about the divorce."

"Yes."

"To-morrow?"

"To-morrow."

Again a slight pause. The moon looked quietly on and there seemed to be a laugh on his broad face. Everything was so quiet, not even a dog was barking.

"Herr Hans!"

"Well, Fräulein Lora?"

"I am in a great hurry to get that divorce." Her voice sounded a little plaintive.

"So am I, Fräulein Lora." And his voice sounded sad.

"You see, there ought not to be any delay."

"No, it is better not to delay."

"The sooner we talk it over the better."

"The better, Fräulein Lora."

"We might talk it over at once."

"If you think so, we will."

"You can come up into my room."

The door opened gently, Hans disappeared within, and presently found himself in Miss Neuman's neat and pleasant room. She wore a white dressing gown and looked very pretty.

"You see, it will cost us a deal of money to get a divorce."

"Do you think anybody can see us from below?"

"No, the windows are dark."

Then began a conversation about the divorce which does not belong to our tale.

Peace returned to Struck Oil City.

Printed in the United States
40053LVS00001B/77